SPOOKSMITHS INVESTIGATE
THE CINDERMAN

Don't expect a warning,
The Cinderman is calling,
Ashes, ashes,
Beware his name!

For Mum and Dad,
thank you for everything.

First published in the UK in 2024 by Usborne Publishing Limited., Usborne House, 83-85 Saffron Hill, London EC1N 8RT, England, usborne.com

Usborne Verlag, Usborne Publishing Ltd., Prüfeninger Str. 20, 93049 Regensburg, Deutschland, VK Nr. 17560

Text copyright © Alex Atkinson, 2024

The right of Alex Atkinson to be identified as the author of this work has been asserted by her in accordance with the Copyright, Designs and Patents Act, 1988.

Cover illustration and map by Miriam Serafin © Usborne Publishing Limited, 2024

The name Usborne and the Balloon logo are Trade Marks of Usborne Publishing Limited.

A CIP catalogue record for this book is available from the British Library.

ISBN 9781835400937   9749/1   JFMAMJJA OND/24

Printed and bound using 100% renewable electricity by CPI Group (UK) Ltd, CR0 4YY

SPOOKSMITHS INVESTIGATE
The CINDERMAN

ALEX ATKINSON

USBORNE

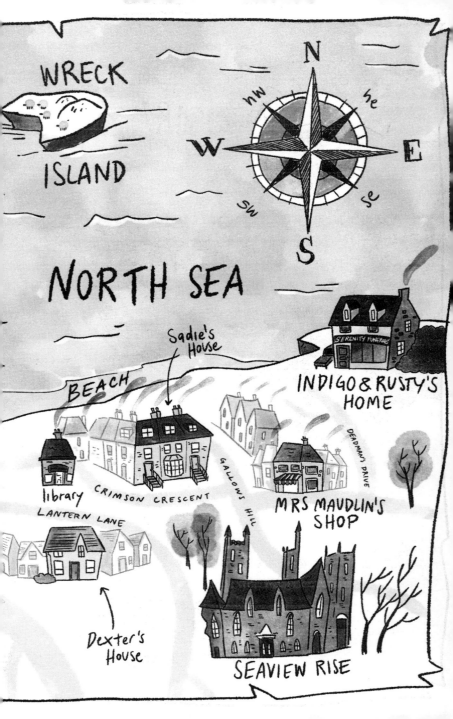

1

Most twelve-year-olds would be creeped-out standing alone in a graveyard at dusk.

I'm not most twelve-year-olds.

Growing up in a funeral home, I know the dead don't come back and ghosts only exist in stories.

I check Dad isn't watching and push further into the long grass, the sweet smell of pollen washed away by the salty sea breeze. Ahead is the cliff top and what remains of Little Hope Church: a crumbling tower surrounded by lichen-covered graves. It's the perfect habitat for one of my favourite animals.

High above my head, a single shadow zigzags through the darkening sky. I freeze, my breath catching in my throat, and listen hard. Most bat calls can only be heard with a special detector, but my hearing seems to be getting better with age. I can make out its high-pitched squeak-clicks above the crash of the waves.

The creature weaves through the air, fast and jerky as it ducks and dives, catching insects on the wing. A single pipistrelle bat can eat up to 3,000 insects in one night. That's the same as a human eating sixty roast dinners in a day. Mind-blowing. Or, in this case, stomach-busting.

Even though I can quote at least another million wildlife facts, Dad thinks my animal obsession is just a phase. No matter how many times I tell him I'm going to be a vet, he thinks I'll eventually join the family business like he did.

Me? A funeral director? I'd rather swallow a spider in my sleep! (That's an urban myth by the way. Snoring scares arachnids away.)

More bats are appearing now, shooting out of the belfry at electrifying speeds. I wade through a patch of ox-eye daisies and sit down, leaning against an unnamed gravestone covered in honeysuckle. I inhale the vanilla scent of the flowers – Grandpa would have been proud I identified them so quickly – and sit back to enjoy the show.

"Indigo?"

Ugh. Dad has remembered me. He's been chatting to the Rev about moving the cliff-top graves to the new churchyard. The Rev doesn't do quick conversations. He took so long over our next-door neighbour's christening I thought baby Harvey would be ready for secondary school before the service was over.

If I'm quiet, maybe the two of them will keep blathering on...

"Indigo!"

Or maybe not.

I sit up.

"Are you there?" Dad shouts.

There's no right answer. He knows I'm in the graveyard. And I know I'm not supposed to be. Something about it being dangerous, but I wasn't really paying attention.

It's best I keep out of sight, so I start crawling back the way I came. At least, I think it's the way I came. It looks different on all fours, long grass hitting me in the face. I nearly impale a hand on some broken railings.

If I can just make it back to the hearse without collecting some *grave* injury (sorry), I can pretend I've been reading something worthy. There's a copy of *From Sibling Rivals to Best Friends* in the car door. The title makes me want to throw up, but Mum's been pushing me to read it ever since she started her counselling course.

My knee crunches down on a sharp stone and I bite my bottom lip to stop from crying out. Crawling hurts. How do babies do it? I'm rubbing my knee better when two heavily polished black shoes stomp down in front of me.

Uh oh.

"Indigo Smith, what do you think you're doing?"

I stand up. The grass and seeds stuck in my hair and all over my tracksuit bottoms tell Dad exactly what I've been doing.

"I cannot believe you ignored me. Again!"

His face is an alarming shade of purple. That, combined with his grey suit makes him look like an angry thundercloud.

"We're moving the graves from this old churchyard for a reason," Dad continues. "It's not safe. Erosion has turned this whole place into a deathtrap!"

Seriously?

"It's a graveyard. Of course it's a deathtrap—"

"Don't get smart with me. In the car. Now!"

My shoulders slump as he strides off, stiff backed. He doesn't get me at all. When Grandpa died of a heart attack three months ago, all Dad's sense of fun and adventure died with him. Sighing, I trail after him, leaving the bats to their twilight dance.

By the time we reach our driveway, I can barely breathe.

The bunch of lilies in the back stink and my nose has been clamped between my fingers for over fifteen minutes.

Without saying a word, I scramble out of the passenger door and suck in a lungful of fresh air.

Our house is one of the oldest in Greyscar. It sits on its own at the far end of the road, a heap of four-hundred-year-old, weather-beaten stone. On one side is a cliff which drops down to the North Sea and on the other is a big yew hedge separating us from the Blessed family next door and the rest of the street.

I think everyone is happy with this arrangement. You see, there are stories about our house – stories about ghosts and ghouls, creeping shadows and bodiless footsteps. I don't believe any of them, but it comes with the territory when you live on a road called Deadman's Drive and your house isn't just a house, but an actual funeral parlour. We even have a black hearse parked in the driveway and gold writing on the big bay window: *Serenity Funerals – A Family Business*.

Dad gets out of the hearse and tosses me the front door keys.

"Put the flowers in the display window and I won't say anything to your mum about you exploring a derelict and dangerous churchyard."

I groan.

"Got something better to do?"

"Yes." I jut my chin out defiantly. "I'm going to Dexter's to see the badgers."

But Dad's already walking towards the back garden, tapping at his phone.

There's no point arguing with someone who refuses to listen. Holding my breath, I collect the flowers from the car and unlock the door to the funeral parlour at the front of the house.

The walls are painted in a soft pink that reminds me of a dog's tongue. Mum says it's "comforting", but any comfort is cancelled out by the gloomy-looking portraits of our gloomy-looking relatives hanging on the walls. They are all equally hideous, apart from the one of Grandpa, all twinkly dark eyes and knowing smile.

I have two work-obsessed parents and a seriously irritating twin brother, Rusty, so Grandpa was the person I shared everything with. The one who encouraged my love of wildlife; who applauded me, aged five, as I identified a dried fox poo; who bought me my first pair of binoculars and taught me that honeysuckle smells like vanilla and that pineapple weed smells like, well, pineapple. I still can't believe that I'll never share anything with him again.

A weight settles on my chest, and I look away from the portraits towards the heavy oak desk in the centre of the room. There's one flowery chair behind it and two in front. A wooden floor-to-ceiling bookcase covers the back wall. It's filled with dusty old books no one touches, just the way it was when Grandpa was head undertaker.

Dad says he's kept it the same because it's reassuring for customers to find things unchanged. I think it's so Dad can still feel close to Grandpa. He lived here with us and taught Dad everything he knows about the business. He even made time to paint horrible Battle Beast models with Rusty and got him one of those fancy airbrush kits last Christmas. Rusty says he can't use it now because the nozzle is jammed, but I don't think the nozzle is the problem. I saw him getting all teary last time he took it out of the box.

Grandpa was here and then he was gone and none of us can move past the massive hole he's left in all our lives.

Tears are welling up now, so I concentrate hard on the coffin catalogues on the coffee table. The top copy shows a grinning man sitting inside a wicker casket – hilarious and grim at the same time. I know it's the kind of thing that would have made Grandpa laugh. Luckily, it works on me too. Feeling better, I lock the front door behind me and shove the flowers on the windowsill. Dad could easily have dealt with the lilies himself, but he seems to enjoy torturing me and Rusty with random tasks. Not that I mind him torturing Rusty...

I'm about to head up to my room to get ready for Dexter's when Beethoven's Fifth Symphony sounds in the hallway. I freeze. It's Dad's ringtone. He answers it: right outside the door to the funeral parlour.

There's no way I'm going out there until he's gone. He'll only give me another job and I'm not missing seeing the badgers at my best friend's house because of some pointless chore.

While I wait for Dad's boring conversation to end, I find myself pulling out a selection of books with titles like *Benedict's History of Undertaking* and *The Life and Times of a Travelling Vicar*. Fascinating. Not. I've no idea why Grandpa wouldn't let anyone touch them.

I replace them and as the last book hits the back of the bookcase, the lights flicker as though in warning. There's a *click* followed by a *creak*. I freeze, staring open-mouthed as a coffin-shaped door swings open in the centre of the bookcase.

There's a secret door in my family's bookcase.

A secret door with steps going down behind it...

It's the entrance to a basement. Or a dungeon. Or maybe

it's a bat cave. I let out a nervous laugh, but I'm more excited than scared. I have so many questions. I could – and probably should – get Mum or Dad, but they'll just tell me it's dangerous and stop me investigating...

Or maybe they already know about the secret door and have kept it hidden? A familiar fizz of anger bubbles in my belly. It would be so typical of them to keep something like this quiet. I can hear their disapproving voices in my head: *It's too dark and dangerous and dirty.*

I'm going in.

The doorway doesn't reach down to the floor like a normal door. It's two shelves up, so I have to climb inside, ducking to avoid the clusters of spider's webs dangling from the ceiling. The light behind me illuminates a set of twisting stone steps. I take a deep breath and immediately regret it: the air in here is stinkier than Rusty's bedroom, like dust mixed with sweaty socks.

Halfway down, the stairs twist to the left, a pillar blocking the light from above. The next step down is in complete darkness. I curse myself for not having my phone on me, but heading back up to get it and being caught by Dad isn't an option, so I keep going, holding the wall to guide me. Maybe there's a light switch further down.

Five more steps and I reach the bottom. There's a faint

whispering sound, but it's probably just the pipes from the house. I take a few hesitant, shuffling steps forward and my outstretched hands brush something cold and metallic. The whispering gets louder as I pick the something up. It's the size of a coffee jar and weighs almost nothing.

Intrigued, I shuffle back to the stairs, towards the light. As I climb, the thing seems to get colder. Icy tendrils numb my hands, climbing up my arms towards my heart, leaving me wondering what could be inside.

I round the corner of the basement stairway and a shaft of light from upstairs lands on my hands.

I'm holding a dented, dusty old urn.

The hairs on the back of my neck prickle.

We've got urns all over the place. Why is this one hidden in a secret basement?

As if in answer, the urn lid rattles.

I scream and instinctively throw the urn away. It lands with a clatter somewhere beneath me. The gasping sound that follows chills me to the bone. It sounds like someone taking their first breath in a long time. Heart pounding, I race up the stairs to the doorway pursued by a dry, ash-choked voice:

"Speak my name."

I'm so freaked out I can barely remember my own name,

but I think...I think that voice came from whatever –
or *whoever* – was in that urn.

Which means only one thing: I can hear the dead.

2

Not only can I hear the dead, I'm also now surrounded by bits of one of them. A swirling cloud of human ash has filled the basement. It's the grossest thing ever, like being trapped in a hoover bag full of flaky skin. What is going on? How can one urn contain so much ash and why is it whirling? The air is thick, my lungs wheezing, panic raking my chest. Choking, I claw my way up the steps. I want to scream but opening my mouth means inhaling more of whoever I've spilled.

After what feels like hours but must only be seconds, I scramble over the threshold back into the funeral parlour, slamming the bookcase door shut behind me. It's a pointless act. The ash has a life of its own. It seeps out around the door and twists away like a whirlwind, filling the room.

Gasping and whole-body trembling, I stumble

towards the window. I push the lilies out of the way and fling it wide open.

As though it's been waiting for this moment, the ash rushes for the window with a triumphant scream. It burns my skin as it blasts past me, roaring its way to freedom, leaving behind a deafening silence and a tang like bonfire smoke.

I gaze around the room wide-eyed, pulse thudding. What just happened? Everything *looks* normal. There's no trace of ash, but my ringing ears and shaking hands tell me I can't have imagined it. I've never dropped an urn of human ashes before, but I'm sure the contents don't usually give orders and fly out the window.

My heart is still hammering when the door handle dips, and Dad pokes his head into the room. For the first time in ages, I'm relieved to see him.

"Dad—" I start eagerly, desperate for someone to give me an explanation for what happened. He holds up a finger, cutting me off, and I notice his mobile clamped to his ear.

His eyebrows knit together as he takes in the open window and the lopsided lilies. He gestures for me to close the window and starts speaking into the phone.

What's just happened is more important than a phone call.

"But, Dad, the bookcase—"

Dad shakes his head. He looks tired, his attention focused on the person at the other end of the call. "Of course, I'm delighted Creep It Real tours is doing well, Miss Chen, and thank you for the offer to 'cut me in' on the profits. However, as I've said hundreds of times before, tours of the funeral parlour are out of the question—"

"The ash!" I try again.

Dad covers the mouthpiece.

"Indigo, I need somewhere quiet to take this call. We can speak later."

Even being attacked by a human ash cloud isn't important enough for him to stop what he's doing. I drop my head. What is the point in even trying to speak to him? He's so wrapped up in the family business, he never makes time to listen to his actual family. Although, I don't know why he puts so much effort into something that doesn't seem to make him happy.

Feeling small, I slip out of the room under the watchful glare of the portraits. I need to find someone who'll listen. I need Mum. I follow the clatter of mugs towards the kitchen.

It's Rusty, the last person on earth I want to see. Ever. We might look alike – dark, curly hair, brown eyes and ugly blue-grey birthmark on our left arms – but we have nothing else in common. He's sitting at the kitchen table, drinking a mug of hot chocolate and painting some hideous Battle Beast monster model.

"What are you looking at, loser?" he says.

The lights flicker as though warning me not to do it, but my fist is already clenched and I thump him on the arm.

"OW!" yells Rusty, overdramatically in my opinion. I didn't hit him that hard.

"Indigo! Russell! Are you two fighting again?" Mum shouts down the stairs.

I drop my fist. "He started it!"

"I don't care who started it. Stop it right now!" Mum yells.

Life is so unfair, but at least I got to watch Rusty squirm at his full name. It's hilarious how much he hates it.

I kick the back of his chair. As soon as he looks up, I mouth the word "Russell".

Rusty's cheeks flush red and he springs up, ready to thump me back with his paint-covered hands. But I'm too fast. I sprint out of the room and upstairs before he can reach me.

Mum is in her room, getting changed for her counselling course. I hover in the doorway.

"Mum, I need to talk to you."

"I'm listening," she says, turning away to button up a brightly coloured shirt.

I open my mouth and all the words I've held in tumble out in a torrent.

"I found a door in the bookcase. It leads down to a basement and I found an urn and I dropped it. The ash spoke to me, ordering me to say its name, and then it escaped out of the window."

Mum has stopped buttoning her shirt and is looking at me like I've sprouted horns. Which is fair enough, I suppose. I sound like I'm spouting fairy tales. I pull the sleeves of my hoodie over my hands, shifting my feet awkwardly in the doorway.

"Say that all again, but slowly this time."

I repeat it, blushing at how unlikely it sounds.

Mum's mouth twitches.

I cross my arms. "I'm not lying, if that's what you think."

"I didn't say you were." She finishes buttoning up her shirt. "Show me."

Two minutes later, I'm standing in the now empty funeral parlour with Mum. Dad has finished his call and is nowhere to be seen. I glare at the bookcase.

"I pulled some books out and pushed them back in and it just opened!" I say, pulling out and slamming back volume after volume. "Stupid thing. Why isn't it working?"

"Like this?" says Mum, joining in.

It doesn't make any difference.

Eventually, I pull all the books off the middle shelves. But the dark panel at the back of the bookcase shows nothing – no edges, hinges or gaps. No matter how hard I thump my fists against the wood, it's like the door was never there.

Just when I think things can't get any worse, my brother appears. I swear he can sense when I'm in trouble.

"Trying to wake the dead?" says Rusty.

Mum clears her throat. "Indigo was telling me she thinks there's a—"

"No. No, I don't." I'm not saying anything with him here. He'll only tease me. I've got no proof, nothing to show that what I'm saying is true. Not even a single flake of ash.

Mum wrinkles her forehead. "But you were adamant. And what about the urn? You said—"

"Forget it," I snap. "I made a mistake."

"*I made a mistake*," mimics Rusty.

"Be nice," warns Mum.

"Who made a mistake?" says Dad.

Great. The whole family is here. I can't deal with this. Thankfully, I've got an excuse.

"I'm late to meet Dexter."

Ignoring Rusty's grin, which says he's delighted I've just made a fool of myself even though he doesn't know the full story, I push past them all into the hallway.

Mum follows, putting one arm on my shoulder and leaning in conspiratorially. "Is this a cry for help? Is it to do with not wanting to go to school tomorrow?"

Mum's training to be a counsellor so she can help people with their problems and comfort the bereaved. I think she's got a long way to go, but tonight her inability to grasp what's really going on could work in my favour.

I sidestep her questions.

"Can we talk about it later? I really do need to get to Dexter's." Just thinking about Dexter Vago makes me feel calmer. He'll listen and he won't judge. That's what best friends are for.

"What about dinner?"

"I'll eat at Dexter's."

She nods. "Sometimes it's easier to work through problems with your friends. We'll talk later, though?" She glances at her watch, eager to get to her course. "Be back by nine o'clock."

I nod, trying not to make any promises I can't keep. Then I grab my phone and slip out before Dad can corner me about the mess I've made of the bookcase. I know what I saw and what I heard, and with Dexter's help I'll make sense of it.

3

I hunch my shoulders against the wind and set off for Dexter's. Usually, I'd take my time and study the birds' nests beneath the eaves of the wonky old fishermen's cottages, or the spiders' webs along the railings at the top of Gallows Hill. Tonight, I've got other things on my mind.

There must be an explanation for the way the ash behaved: a draught blowing up from the basement maybe... But that doesn't explain the way it all shot out the window or that creepy voice. And what was that underground room? And where did the door go?

Thumping footsteps interrupt my thoughts. I stop, turning to see Rusty powering towards me.

"Dad tried to get *me* to put back the books *you* pulled out! What were you doing?"

I ignore his question. There's no way I'm telling him anything.

"Tell Dad I'll put them back later."

Rusty puts his hands on his hips. "He wants them all in numbered order."

Any calm I had left has now evaporated. My skin is literally itching with annoyance.

"Fine," I snap. "I'll put them back in numbered order. Later."

"Colour co-ordinated too," Rusty adds.

"You've got to be joking!"

Rusty grins at me. "Got you."

There is literally no one else in the world who can make my blood boil like my brother. Every bone in my body wants to fight back, but it will eat into my time with Dexter. So instead I become the bigger person. I take a deep breath and storm off, hoping that's an end to it. He doesn't take the hint. The thump of his big feet and his heavy breathing are still behind me. I stop again.

"I told you I'd sort it out later," I growl. "Why are you following me?"

"As if I'd follow you by choice." He wrinkles his nose as though the idea disgusts him. "I'm going to the shop to get some sweets. I've got a Battle Beast tournament to prep for."

"Get a life," I mutter under my breath, striding away.

"As if *you*'ve got one," Rusty shouts after me. "Badger botherer!"

"Just leave me alone!" I yell, turning off Deadman's Drive onto Gallows Hill, away from Rusty.

This time he doesn't follow, and I let out a long breath. I just need some space to think. A bit of quiet to decide how I'm going to explain everything to Dexter without it sounding—

Oh no, now Sadie Miller's at the other end of the street, waving at me.

"Indi! Wait up!"

I've told her to call me Indigo. She only arrived in town a few weeks ago, all the way from sunny California. Something about coming back to her mum's hometown after her dad left. I know I should make more of an effort, but I'm finding her presence annoying. The fact that she seems determined to befriend Dexter, *my* best friend since for ever, has nothing to do with it.

Sadie catches me up. She's wearing a white skirt and top, long blond ponytail bouncing excitedly over one shoulder. I'm in dark colours with even darker hair. She's my opposite in every way and I acknowledge her with a grunt.

"Didn't you hear me?"

"Too windy," I lie.

I hurry on with my head down, hoping she'll go away. She doesn't.

"You can say that again," says Sadie in her LA drawl. "Your hair's wild!"

I slap a hand to my head, attempting to flatten my flyaway curls. They spring back out as soon as I remove it.

I really hope Sadie's mum has just sent her out to get some milk and that Dexter hasn't...

"It's so nice of Dexter to invite me along tonight."

Why, Dexter, why? Tonight, of all nights, I need to speak to him alone.

"These badger creatures he was talking about sound super cool," continues Sadie. "I can't wait to meet one in person."

I stop walking.

"You can't 'meet' a badger," I snap, but then I notice her face fall and I feel bad.

"They're wild animals," I add, less harshly this time. "If we're quiet, we can watch them, but there's no way we can get close enough to touch them."

"Totally." She says it like she gets it, but I know she doesn't. Her face looks so eager though. I hope I'm not going to regret this...

"I can fill you in on anything you need to know."

"Count me in!" says Sadie. "I've got so much to learn about all your animals, your traditions and this whole town." She stares at the hulking grey pile of bricks on our left.

It was once the Ashford Asylum, empty for years before it was converted into flats and renamed Seaview Rise. The new name is a cheap disguise though, because the place looks as cosy as Dracula's castle. It's all thin windows, tall chimneys and pointy turrets.

"I can't understand who'd want to live in it," I say.

"Have you heard the story about the girl who died there?" she says.

"Lots of people died there," I say. "We covered it in Year Six. It sounds a terrifying place to have been locked up."

"Some of them weren't even ill, just unwanted. Can you imagine?"

I really don't want to debate Victorian rights and wrongs right now, so I change the subject.

"You seem to know a lot for someone who's only just arrived."

Sadie shrugs. "What can I say? I love stories and legends – the scarier the better. Miss Chen's Creep It Real tour was brilliant."

I snort. Miss Chen is notorious for making things up to bring her tours to life. Although you can't exactly blame her for trying. Old Greyscar's morbid street names, asylum, abandoned graveyard, boarded-up mine and higher than average bat population scream "creep factor" if you haven't grown up here.

Dad thinks Miss Chen's infatuation with ghosts is a little ghoulish. She's always on at him to let her visit the funeral parlour, convinced she'll find proof of the Blasted Banshee or "Chuckles" the Phantom Toddler. As if she'll convince Dad.

"I've done the tour twice already," Sadie continues. "Once on my own and once with Dexter."

"You went on a Creep It Real tour with Dexter?" I splutter.

"Yeah. Last week. Miss Chen taught us that seriously spooky nursery rhyme. You know, the one about the Cinderman?"

Everyone in the North knows it. It's our version of "Ring a Ring o' Roses". Sadie sings it high and loud:

Don't expect a warning,

The Cinderman is calling,

Ashes, ashes,

Beware his name!

"I said we should ask you along," says Sadie. "But Dexter said you hate all that spooky stuff."

"Yeah, well, that's because it's a load of rubbish," I mutter, but I can't help thinking about the secret room, the ash and that voice. Although I'd be more likely to spend a day playing Battle Beast than share all that with Sadie.

Dexter and I always do everything together. I don't get the point of ridiculously expensive, made-up ghost tours, but if he'd really wanted company, I'd have gone with him.

If he'd asked.

I feel a flash of anger at the thought that they've been hanging out without me. Dexter might like the odd ghost tour, but his real passion is animals, same as me. That's how we met. We were in different reception classes, but we both volunteered to look after the school rabbit, Captain Carrot. We've been friends ever since. Best friends. And no American new girl is going to mess that up.

By the time we reach Dexter's house on Troutbeck Drive, I've got a plan. All I have to do is show Sadie how little she has in common with us, and she'll be gone. Meet a badger? She has no idea that it's not that easy. Hours of sitting out in the dark and the cold waiting for one to appear should see her off.

I knock on the freshly painted blue door. Dexter's house is nice and normal. It's on an estate in New Greyscar, all straight lines, clean red bricks and matching designs. No funeral parlours, hidden basements or human ashes here.

"Welcome, fellow nature enthusiasts!" says Dexter,

throwing the door open and giving a little bow. He's got a flair for the dramatic which, come to think of it, is probably how Sadie persuaded him to take that tour.

"Hi, hi, hi!" squeaks Sadie, in a totally over-the-top excited voice. It's so high I swear it could pop a balloon.

I smile and step inside, slipping off my shoes before I go any further. Dexter's house is small and spotless. A bit like him.

"Is that Indigo?" Alice, one of Dexter's mums, yells from the sitting room.

"Hi, Alice," I shout back. "How's the table tennis going?"

"Next time you're over, we need a rematch. Your name's been top of the leader board in this house for too long!"

"Why not this time?" I shout back.

"Bit busy," Alice shouts back cryptically.

Alice is usually super friendly – she's the nicest teacher at Saltburn Academy, although I have to call her Ms Vago there. It's not her style to miss an opportunity to say hi and insist on a quick game. I look at Dexter.

Dexter rolls his eyes. "Mum T's out, so Mum A is having a *Ghostbusters* movie marathon."

"And it's got to the good bit where Slimer appears," yells Alice. "So help yourself to anything you want, just leave me in peace. Unless, you know, your head falls off or something."

"I love *Ghostbusters*!" says Sadie.

I'm about to suggest she stays in and watches the movies so I can talk to Dexter about the secret room and the weird ash, ALONE, when he ushers us through to the kitchen. Once we're in there, I'm distracted by my name at the top of the chalkboard. I didn't know I was any good at table tennis until the Vagos got me playing in the summer holidays, but seeing it up there makes me smile. If that doesn't show Sadie just how close I am to Dexter and his family, nothing will.

"Mum T made white chocolate chip cookies for pudding," says Dexter. "And there's soup in a Thermos for our main course."

"What are we waiting for?" I ask. Sadie doesn't look like she has any intention of joining the movie marathon, so I'm eager to get her outside so she can get bored and cold and go home. Then, finally, I might get a chance to talk to Dexter about what's really on my mind.

"I've got a hide set up at the end of the garden," says Dexter, opening the patio door. "The badgers will be out soon. Come on."

Sadie and I grab our shoes and follow him out. The badger sett, or den, is in the field at the end of his garden. I've seen the badgers tons of times and it's always magical, but tonight I'd swap seeing them for half an hour of Dexter's time minus

Sadie. If I keep this secret in, it feels like it will eat me up from the inside.

As we walk to the end of Dexter's long thin garden, Sadie steps on several twigs, creating a symphony of snaps and cracks guaranteed to send any animal running. Yet more proof Sadie doesn't belong. I smile to myself.

The definition of a hide is a camouflaged shelter to watch wildlife from; Dexter's version is an old play tent with a bit of camo netting thrown over the top.

"You guys were loud," he whispers, as we squeeze inside.

I grin, pleased he noticed. "It's not my fault Sadie walks like Bigfoot," I reply.

"I couldn't see what I was stepping on," argues Sadie. "Haven't you guys heard of flashlights?"

"They're called torches and they have a tendency to scare wild animals away." I say it slowly to make sure she gets the "duh" in my voice.

"If your bickering doesn't do it first," hisses Dexter.

We all fall silent and shuffle up uncomfortably around the torn plastic window, shoulders touching, eyes slowly adjusting to the dark.

The peace lasts about a minute.

"I know we're supposed to be being quiet, but someone has to say it…"

Do they, Sadie?

"...we're in the dark, in a tent – this is the perfect spot for a ghost story. Have you heard the one about the Blasted Banshee—"

"Mine accident. Big flood. Dead kid. Devastated mother swears to haunt Greyscar for ever. The end."

It's a well-known story round here – not that I believe in the ghostly elements, obviously.

"What about the library ghosts?" she says.

"Stop going on about ghosts!" I snap.

Sadie takes a breath as though she's about to say something and then she turns away. There's a flapping sound as she fights her way out of the camo netting and storms off.

"That was out of order," says Dexter.

I'm glad it's dark because I blush.

"I don't know why she's here. She's clearly more interested in ghosts than animals."

"Have you ever thought that it's not about the animals?" says Dexter. "She's moved from the other side of the world and she's probably lonely. She's just trying to make friends."

I hadn't thought of that. I'd just thought about how she'd got in the way of my friendship with Dexter. My cheeks flush hotter.

"You need to go after her and apologize," says Dexter.

"But I need to talk to you," I say weakly. "And what about the badgers? And the soup? And the cookies?"

"No badgers, soup or cookies until you've made things right with Sadie."

He glares at me, and I hang my head, then duck under the netting and stomp back down the garden. Badgers fight to defend their territory and I've just seen off an interloper. So why do I feel so bad about it? Curse my human conscience.

By the time I reach the house, the side gate is open and Sadie is gone.

Something soft as a feather brushes against my nose in the darkness. I wipe it off with my sleeve and hurry after Sadie.

It's not until I'm standing beneath a street light at the end of Troutbeck Drive that I notice the grey smear on my black coat where I rubbed my nose. It carries with it a smoky burnt sort of smell.

My heart skips a beat.

It looks and smells like ash. But it can't be, can it?

4

I stare at the ashy mark on my coat and the words to that nursery rhyme crawl inside my head:

Don't expect a warning,

The Cinderman is calling,

Ashes, ashes,

Beware his name!

It's a song for little kids. I hadn't thought of it in years before Sadie started singing it.

The street lights flicker and a blurry white figure appears at the end of Saltburn Street.

"Sadie?" I call.

The figure turns the corner onto Coal Road, and I shake my head. If it is Sadie, she's going the wrong way home.

Guilt prickles my conscience and I sprint after her. Dexter was the first proper friend I ever made and I guess I'm not used to sharing him. It's never been a problem before because no one's been interested in joining our group. It's not Sadie's fault her timing sucks. She doesn't know that I found a secret room and creepy talking ash and need my best friend more than ever.

Soon I'm standing alone on Coal Road, right on the edge of New Greyscar, beside the wasteland.

It's dark, but I can make out the railings and gates strung with bright yellow *DANGER! KEEP OUT!* signs ahead. Greyscar House and Greyscar Mine are on the other side, or so I'm told. I've never seen them. Most of the house is rumoured to have collapsed into the mining tunnels beneath it. Miss Chen is always trying to get permission to go in. She's got a million and one ghost stories about both the mine and the house. The more superstitious townsfolk say they are cursed and won't talk about them at all.

I peer harder into the gloom. The lights of Oldcastle Steelworks should be blazing in the distance, creating an orange glow on the horizon. But tonight, there are no lights other than the street lights behind me. No lights out at sea either. It's as if a blanket has been thrown over Greyscar, cutting us off from the outside world.

I shiver and shake my head.

"Get a grip," I say aloud, my voice faltering as a white flash catches the corner of my eye.

There's a figure at the bottom of Coal Road, near Bat Lane.

"Sadie!" I shout.

She ignores me, disappearing through the gates to Little Hope Graveyard.

By the time I reach the gates, the moon has emerged, illuminating the tombs. They peep above the long grass like waiting sharks and a faint vanilla scent drifts towards me on the cool night air. Where has she gone?

"Boo!"

I scream and spin around to find a familiar face grinning back at me.

"Rusty!" I yell, my heart pounding so hard I feel sick. I swipe at him, but he jumps back, out of reach. "What are you doing here?"

"I called in on Jai and what did I hear when I left? The sweet song of a nightingale? The soft coo of a pigeon? No. It was you, screeching."

I know some people love having a twin but maybe that's because their sibling is kind and supportive, unlike Rusty. I shiver at the thought of having some kind of psychic twin connection with him. It would be like being permanently trolled.

"Yeah, well, I wasn't calling for you."

Rusty does a high-pitched impression of me calling for Sadie. He makes me sound like a yowling cat.

"I don't sound like that!"

"You do actually," says Rusty.

"At least I've got friends to lose," I reply.

"At least my friends don't run away from me."

Rusty's words hit home, and I clench and unclench my jaw. I haven't treated Sadie like a friend. It's no wonder she ran away from me. I wish I could hit rewind and take it all back, but I can't and now I'm going to have to live with the consequences. For tonight at least, I'm going to have to keep the ash, the voice and the secret room to myself.

I don't have Sadie's number, but I do have Dexter's. Turning away from Rusty so he can't snoop, I type Dexter a quick message:

Looked everywhere but can't find Sadie. TMR, I'll apologize. Promise I'll fix this. I'm sorry. Don't h8 me.

I put my phone away, aware that Rusty is staring at me.

"What's really going on?"

"I don't want to talk about it," I say, retracing my steps up Bat Lane before turning onto Full Moon Cove. I can hear Rusty behind me, but maybe he's as fed up as I am, because he doesn't try to start anything for once.

Tonight has been an utter disaster. All I want is to crawl

into my bed and wake up to a new day and a chance to put things right.

I'm not feeling my most sparky, so it takes me a while to notice that the streets are completely empty, which is odd even for eight o'clock on a Sunday evening. I can't quite put my finger on it, but it's a bit like the calm before a storm. I can't shake the feeling that something is out there, waiting and watching.

The sea is singing *hush* as it rushes up and down the beach. I don't feel hushed. I feel unsettled – my palms are clammy and my skin is itchy, but I've got no one to tell. Rusty doesn't count. I try not to notice the ghost tour posters plastered to the sides of the Creep It Real hut and the dark windows of the usually bustling Ship Inn.

After what feels like for ever, we reach home. I'm greeted by a loud, angry squawk. It's Phrank, an escapee pheasant from the local shoot. He lives in our hedge and usually only attacks customers and the postwoman. We have a special bond, mainly because I'm the one who feeds him.

"It's me!" I shout.

Phrank's having none of it. He puffs out his chest and I stifle a scream as he flies up at my face, wings wide, talons bared.

But Phrank isn't aiming at me.

With a flap he's up and over my head, landing behind

me, squawking and caw-cawing.

"Phrank! Cut it out!" Rusty yells. But he's not aiming at Rusty either. It's like there's something behind my twin, something we can't see but Phrank can.

As I stab at the lock with my key, the security light finally clicks on, the warm glare of home chasing the night away.

"Did your face scare Phrank? Is that why he's shrieking?" asks Rusty, catching me up.

"Bog off," I say, finally getting the key in the lock.

I open the door.

"Losers first," I grumble, as Rusty barges past me.

I hang up my coat and go back into the funeral parlour to put the books away. I shove them back in any old order. There's still no sign of the doorway in the bookcase, but I don't want to be in here a moment longer than I need to after all the weird stuff that's happened today.

When I step back out into the hallway, Rusty's walking through eating a slice of pizza. He's wearing a black Battle Beast T-shirt with a green three-headed monster dripping blood on the front. It's almost enough to put me off dinner. Almost.

"Where did you get that?"

"Kitchen," he grunts, with a full mouth.

There's takeaway pizza on the kitchen table with a note from Mum saying to help ourselves. I grab a couple of slices and head up to my room, relieved that Rusty's already gone to his. I can hear him yabbering on about some Battle Beast character to Jai on his headset.

It's hard to believe we're related. Although, until about six months ago, Rusty and I were okay. I mean, not besties or anything – who would want to be best friends with their brother? – but we had a more tolerant, not-rip-into-each-other-at-every-opportunity relationship. Then Grandpa died, and we both left primary school, and over the summer holidays Rusty morphed into this Battle Beast obsessed, stinky gargoyle.

I shove the rest of my slice of pizza in my mouth and yank the curtains closed. All I want right now is to shut the world out, and everyone in it. Not only have I messed everything up with Sadie and Dexter, but there's something seriously strange going on – and I'm trying NOT to think about the secret room under this house and what came out of it.

Climbing under the duvet and reading for a bit might stop my mind racing. I've just got to deal with the carefully folded carrier bag on my bed first. There's a pink Post-it note stuck to it covered in Mum's familiar, loopy handwriting.

I saw this and thought of you. It's got lots of pockets for your wildlife paraphernalia :)

I pick up the bag. It feels squishy and I have a horrible feeling it may contain...clothes.

Yep.

Mum has bought me clothes.

Now there's a sentence that strikes fear into my heart. Mum's always trying to get me to dress "jazzier", but if I dress the way she wants me to, I'll scare off all the wildlife between here and Oldcastle.

I take a deep breath, reach into the bag and pull out a neon yellow boiler suit with rainbow cuffs. Looking at it makes me want to wear sunglasses. I chuck the boiler suit under my bed to join the pea-green shirt with the high neck AND the revolting floaty skirt with embroidered flowers. Then I pick up my phone.

A reply is waiting for me from Dexter.

I don't h8 you.

I smile, instantly feeling less edgy. I prop myself up on the bed and text him back.

I really am sorry. I will make things right with Sadie.

I know, he replies. *Gotta go, Mum A's eating all the cookies!*

The thought of food makes my stomach rumble – I missed out on soup and cookies at Dexter's. I go downstairs and help myself to more pizza.

Luckily, I don't bump into any of my family on the way. Dad is a complete workaholic and is always hunched over his paperwork on a Sunday and Rusty is glued to a screen.

Back in my room I pick up a copy of *Zoology* and read until I'm yawning.

I switch off the light as I hear Mum come in the front door and up the stairs. I really can't face that "talk" she promised me, so I burrow further under the duvet. She pauses outside my room, opening my door a crack. I make sure to breathe heavily and rhythmically, like I'm asleep. It must convince Mum, because the door clicks shut again, and her footsteps move away.

I try to sleep for real after that, but when I shut my eyes, I'm back in the basement, ash choking my lungs, the door to the funeral parlour just out of reach.

I open my eyes and flick the light back on, staring at my flying-unicorn patterned curtains. The horned beasts have been given cheery grins by a designer who obviously got carried away. They are deeply offensive and way too babyish for a twelve-year-old, but this isn't what gets to me tonight.

Tonight, it's the gap in the curtains where the two halves don't quite meet. My eyes are drawn to the sliver of night peeping through. Even when I turn my back, it feels like the darkness is watching me.

5

My eyes feel dry and tired, as if I've been keeping watch all night. I squint at my alarm clock.

00:00

That can't be right. It's daylight outside.

I check my phone. It's dead. Great. I huff and sit up, plugging it into the charger beside my bed, listening for creaking floorboards and groaning pipework: noises that say Mum's getting dressed, Dad's in the shower and the day has started.

Nothing.

Don't tell me I'm late for school again. I groan. Mondays suck. Why didn't anyone wake me?

Grudgingly, I climb out of my warm bed and into my cold uniform – grey trousers, white shirt and hideous red jumper. It's not until I'm trying to wrestle my unruly curls into a clip that I realize just how quiet it is.

The seagulls should be screeching; Mr Blessed next door should be revving his car to take Harvey to nursery and the postwoman should be yelling at Phrank to "Get off!"

But there's no screeching, or revving, or shouting.

I listen harder.

It's a special sort of quiet, the smothering sort, like when it snows. But snow? In September?

Pushing aside the curtains, I stare out of the window and my breath catches in my throat.

The world as I know it has vanished.

Phrank's hedge; the red-and-white-striped awning of Mrs Maudlin's corner shop; the rooftops of Fisherman's End and the turrets of the old asylum – everything, as far as I can see, is coated in a layer of grey dust. Even the sea is covered in a grey haze.

Hands shaking, I open the window and lean out.

Greyscar is as quiet as a grave and looks like an old black-and-white film. Wide-eyed, I scan the streets, inhaling a smokiness that sticks to the back of my throat. Two men wearing top hats are standing where Deadman's Drive meets Gallows Hill, but when I blink and look back, the men have gone. Odd. I rub my eyes, focusing on a flock of seagulls battling their way out to sea through the haze. Right about now they should be dive-bombing the fish market. Instead, they're making their escape.

Skin tingling with unease, I run a finger along the now grey and gritty windowsill. It looks and smells ashy. My unease turns to panic.

"Mum!" I shout. "Dad!"

I run out onto the landing, thundering down the stairs into the kitchen to find Mum and Dad sitting at the table in silence.

"There's been an accident," I blurt.

"Accident?" says Dad, looking up from his coffee, blinking like he's waking from a daydream.

Why's he so calm? Dad's never calm, especially not on a school morning when he's trying to get me and Rusty out the door. Maybe it's some new chilled parenting technique Mum's taught him from her course? I cross the room in three strides and throw open the door.

"Look. Look out there! It's an environmental disaster!"

I point to the grey garden, expecting sounds of shock, but Dad just stares out of the open doorway with an odd sort of detachment.

"No cause for alarm," says Mum, not even bothering to turn around to look. "Only an incident at the steelworks."

She takes a bite of her toast and smiles up at me.

"An 'incident'?" I say. "It must have been a pretty big 'incident'."

Mum leans over and switches on the radio. I try not to groan as it fizzes and whines searching for a signal. Mum insists on using the silly old thing even though both Rusty and I have told her a smart speaker with Alexa would be so much easier.

As Mum adjusts the aerial for the hundredth time, I notice how grey and tired-looking she is; even her brightly coloured shirt looks subdued, like the colours have been washed out. I'm making a mental note to give her a break with the hating-my-brother thing, when an old-fashioned voice crackles into the room over the radio.

An ash cloud has settled on Greyscar after an incident at Oldcastle Steelworks. There is no cause for alarm. Continue your day as normal... An ash cloud has settled on Greyscar after an incident at Oldcastle Steelworks. There is no cause for alarm. Continue your day as normal...

It's a dry, ash-choked voice that demands attention, wiggling its way inside my head like an earworm. It sounds familiar, but everything is so freaky right now I can't remember where I've heard it before. The message repeats several times before I slam my hand on the off button.

"See? No cause for alarm," says Dad, brow furrowed like he's concentrating overly hard on thinking.

The message makes everything *sound* as though it's under control. Mum and Dad seem convinced, but I'm not so sure. Where's the normal, chirpy newsreader?

Rusty enters the kitchen, scratching his belly with one hand and picking his nose with the other.

So far, so normal.

"What's 'no cause for alarm'?" he asks, examining a bogey on the end of his finger.

Seriously gross. I'd be more than happy to teach him some manners, but right now I need him on my side.

"See for yourself," I say, opening the door.

He shuffles over, all sleepy and dopey-looking. But as soon as he sees the ash, his face loses that jowly, crumpled look, and his eyes widen.

"What is that stuff?"

I flick the radio back on, allowing the message to repeat twice before I turn it off.

"Does this mean school's shut?" asks Rusty, shoulders round his ears and a nervous edge to his voice. "Because Battle Beast Club is meeting in the art room tonight. Jai says I've got no killer instinct, so I have to be there to try out some new moves before Friday's tournament."

Typical of Rusty to only think about himself and Battle Beast when the town's half-buried in ash.

Dad puts two slices of bread in the toaster. His hands shake. "Continue your day as normal," he says.

Rusty lowers his shoulders.

"Well then, if everything is normal..." He grabs a bowl, filling it to the brim with Wheatie Hoops, before plonking himself down at the table.

"Does no one want to talk about what's happening?" I ask.

Three blank faces stare back at me. Milk dribbles down Rusty's chin.

Everyone else seems to be okay with the scene outside. And the radio message. Maybe the uneasy niggle in my belly is hunger after all? I pull out a chair, sit down and unwrap a brioche.

I'm onto my second brioche and have almost convinced myself I might be overreacting, when black smoke starts pouring from the toaster.

"Toast!" I cry, spraying chewed bread all over the table.

"No cause for alarm," says Dad.

I jump up, pop the toaster and open the door, wafting it to clear the smoke.

Rusty wrinkles his nose but makes no effort to help. It's typical of him, but not of Mum and Dad. Neither of them moves a muscle. What is going on?

Burning toast is one of the quickest ways to rile Dad. We've been told a million times that no one wants to visit a funeral parlour and smell burning. That's why we have stinky lilies and lavender air freshener everywhere. But this morning neither he nor Mum reacts – it's like they're zombified or something. And what's even weirder is that they then eat the cremated bread.

I clear my throat, trying to get Rusty's attention. He's too busy shovelling cereal into his mouth to notice.

"Time for school," Mum and Dad suddenly announce in perfect unison, their smiles black with burnt toast crumbs.

I don't know how they know it's time because the oven clock is flashing crazily – there must have been a power cut – but maybe grown-ups have an in-built alarm for these things.

Today though, it plays into my hands. I'm desperate to get Rusty away from Mum and Dad so I can talk to him about them. The radio message is blaming the ash outside on the steelworks, but nothing can explain our parents' behaviour.

"Let's go," I say.

Rusty lifts his head and frowns. "I haven't finished."

"I'll buy you something on the way."

He frowns. "Why would you do that?"

"Because I'm nice," I hiss, feeling about as nice as a King Cobra.

He narrows his eyes. "What do you want?"

I ball my fists. He's really testing my patience.

"Can't a girl do something for her brother without wanting something in return?"

"No."

"I'll buy you crisps. Chocolate. Whatever you want," I try.

Mum jerks her head at the mention of chocolate and crisps, but she doesn't take it any further. Where's the lecture about eating a proper breakfast?

"Fine," says Rusty, finally standing up. "You'd better cough up because I'm hungry and I'm out of cash. Maintaining a full Battle Beast Battalion is expensive. I used up everything I had to buy a new Kombat Kill Krew for the tournament."

WOW. I have no idea how he can spend every spare second of his life painting little plastic models to battle other people's little plastic models like a total loser. But he's all I've got right now.

"Later, Mum. Later, Dad," I murmur.

At the mention of their names, Mum and Dad look up simultaneously.

"Continue your day as normal," they chorus.

I bundle Rusty out of the door.

As soon as it clicks shut behind us, I turn to him. "Do you really not notice anything different about Mum and Dad this morning?"

"The only one acting 'different' is you," he says sulkily.

He kicks the ground and a smoky cloud billows into the air, surrounding me in swirling ash...like when I dropped the urn...

I push the thought away. It was a small urn, a teaspoonful compared to what's covering Greyscar. The radio says there was an accident at the steelworks. Besides, the ash isn't my most pressing problem...

I look back towards the house. Our parents are standing at the window, watching us.

I wave and they both jerkily sweep their hands back and forth across the windowpane. They make it look as though waving is a movement they've never done before.

That uneasy feeling stirs in my belly again.

"Let's go," I say to Rusty.

"Best thing you've said all morning." He pushes past me and strides out of the garden.

I pause only to check on Phrank. What if he's left like the seagulls? I peer into the yew hedge, relieved to find him eyeing me back.

"I don't know what's going on, Phranky, but I'm going to get to the bottom of this," I whisper.

6

A town blanketed in ash, parents acting unparenty and a creepy radio announcement. It's not necessarily the end of the world, but let's just say I'm not my usual easy-going self.

"Come on! I'll die if I don't eat something soon!" Rusty yells.

"I'll kill you if you don't shut up about eating something soon," I mutter, hurrying after him, footsteps muffled by the ash.

It's not until we reach the corner shop that I realize we haven't passed a single other person or animal. No cats creeping around corners or dogs pulling at their leads. No birds or birdsong either.

I hand Rusty some cash and he goes inside Mrs Maudlin's corner shop, setting the doorbell jingling. It's a reassuringly ordinary sound and I take a deep breath, trying to calm my nerves. It doesn't help. The air is clogged with the scent of smoke, making me cough and splutter.

If it's doing this to me, what's it doing to the wildlife? Why are we being told to carry on as normal? Surely, we should be doing something or, at the very least, staying at home until this mess is sorted out. Where are the clean-up teams? The emergency services? Greenpeace?

I move out from beneath the once red-and-white-striped awning, scanning the streets for signs of life.

They're still deserted and eerily quiet. This is the biggest thing to happen in Greyscar since for ever and no one is here. No reporters from the local newspaper or TV crews and, most surprising of all, no Miss Chen announcing it's all a ghost conspiracy on her Creep It Real loudspeaker.

I don't even know if we are late, but I want to get to school because I suddenly feel the need to see other people, specifically Dexter. He always has an explanation for everything.

I stamp my foot. What is Rusty doing in there?

He finally emerges, tucking into a KitKat Chunky, and I stride off, shouting, "Come on!" over my shoulder.

Rusty catches me up on Gallows Hill, his red school jumper peppered with slivers of chocolate and wafer because of the messy way he eats. However, now that he's eaten, maybe he'll pay attention. I try again.

"We need to talk. Mum and Dad—"

"There's nothing wrong with Mum and Dad," he snaps.

I've definitely hit a nerve.

I push on. "Really? When have you known Dad not to kick off about burning toast? Or Mum to let you have chocolate for breakfast without a row?"

He shrugs and looks at his feet in a way that says he doesn't want to engage. I'm not letting him get off that easily. "What about the ash and that radio message?"

"There was an accident at the steelworks."

"You believe that?"

"Why wouldn't I?"

I'm so frustrated I could scream. "Where is everyone then, genius? The whole place is deserted."

"No, it's not," says Rusty, a note of triumph in his voice. "Mrs Maudlin was in her shop. Everyone else will be around here somewhere. Look at all the footprints."

He's right. I can't believe I didn't notice them before. There are loads of footprints in the ash.

"Know your problem?" says Rusty.

"You?"

He ignores me. "Sticking your nose in where it doesn't belong."

I shake my head. Not only do I think we're not related, I also think he might not be from this planet.

"What you don't see can't hurt you," he adds, which is a load of rubbish.

I'm sure he wasn't always this unobservant. It's as though part of him has shut down since Grandpa died. Like it has with Dad.

"So you think it's best just to pretend you don't see stuff? Don't question things?"

"Works for me." Rusty pulls a packet of crisps out of his pocket and pops it open with a bang. It's gunshot-loud and I automatically check over my shoulder. My instincts are telling me to stay small and hidden, but that message obviously isn't getting through to Rusty.

He walks ahead, noisily crunching his crisps. Keeping my distance, I follow, retracing our usual route to school. Except today, there doesn't seem to be anything usual about it.

The curve of Crimson Crescent seems less of a gentle arc and more like the houses are hunching their backs against me; the pink rose garden in front of Seaview Rise Apartments is dull, deadened by the fallen ash.

By the time we reach Saltburn Academy, the playground is empty, although the ash is all smudged and trodden down like students and teachers have passed through.

"They must be in class," I say.

"Thanks for stating the obvious, Sherlock."

Thank goodness Rusty and I are in separate classes, because I'd be struggling not to thump him every five minutes. He's been no help. I can't wait to find Dexter and get his opinion on all this weirdness.

We hurry across the playground and into the main building. Whoever designed Saltburn Academy had no imagination. It's made up of four separate blocks containing two storeys of square classrooms, plus a gym and a library. It is easily the most boring building in Greyscar.

Inside it's unusually quiet and, although all the lights are on, it's dimly lit as though the bulbs aren't working properly. I cross the hallway, skirting a cold spot by the radiator – what is wrong with the heating in this place? – and shove my bag in my locker. It's history first and Alice – I mean Ms Vago – is covering Mr Trevathan's parental leave.

"Thanks for breakfast," says Rusty, before adding, "Bye, loser," as he disappears down the corridor.

Sometimes, I really do think I hate him.

The history classroom is in the next block over, near the library. Ignoring the *NO RUNNING IN THE HALLS* signs, I jog back outside and round the side of the building. Although I should be safe from a telling-off with Dexter's mum. Ms Vago will just give me a wink and tell me to sit down.

I push the door to 7T open. The lights are off in the classroom, but the seats are full, red Saltburn Academy jumpers sticking out in the gloom like hazard lights. Everyone is staring straight ahead, concentrating intently on something, although there's nothing on the board. I must be really late, and I've missed the explanation. Ms Vago doesn't look up and everyone else is so deeply into whatever it is they're doing they haven't even noticed me arriving.

Feeling hot and flustered, I slide into a plastic chair, one row back and two seats away from Dexter. His ironed jumper gives him away.

"Psst," I hiss, trying to get his attention.

He doesn't react, so I rip a corner off the blank sheet of paper on my desk, ball it up and throw it at him.

It bounces off his neck, but he doesn't turn around.

Don't tell me he's still mad at me about the Sadie stuff!

It's then that I notice Sadie is sitting in my seat, next to Dexter, her blond hair dull and pulled into an unshowy low ponytail.

There's a sharp stab of realization.

Are they freezing me out?

Then, as though they've received a signal, everyone picks up their pens and starts writing.

My heart starts to beat faster. Is this another test I've forgotten to revise for?

On all sides, every student is scribbling away as though they're possessed. How do they know what to do?

There's no avoiding it.

I put up my hand.

"Yes?" says Ms Vago.

Her voice sounds hoarse and gravelly, like she's got a bad cold.

"What is everyone writing?" My voice echoes in the quiet.

Slowly, Ms Vago gets to her feet and begins to write on the interactive white board. The only sound is the squeak of her pen.

While I wait, I stare at the back of Dexter and Sadie's heads. I want to apologize to Sadie and Dexter knows it. Why is he ignoring me? And how does he know what to write? It's all properly weird.

Ms Vago steps back from the board and all thoughts of Dexter and Sadie are pushed from my mind. There must be some mistake, because written in black pen isn't a history assignment, or even a question – it's a list of rules:

1. *Listen carefully.*

2. *Do not resist.*

3. *Wait for orders.*

Seriously? Do not resist? I give a nervous smile, but it quickly falls away. No one else seems to think it's remotely funny, least of all Ms Vago, who fixes me with a stare that could freeze a heatwave.

Outside, further down the corridor, I hear the jangle of keys and the clunk of locks.

Are we being locked in?

My legs are quivering now, my knees jumping up and down. I can't ignore it. It isn't all in my imagination – my body is telling me to run.

I say the first thing that comes into my head: "I need the loo!"

It's not one of my best excuses, but I'm on my feet and out the door before Ms Vago can answer.

Mr Cane, the headmaster, is two classrooms away, carrying a huge set of keys. He's a tall, thin man with a bushy moustache that reminds me of a hairy caterpillar. When someone wears what looks like an insect on their top lip it makes it quite hard to take them seriously, but today I don't find it even remotely amusing. Mr Cane locks the door of 8F, his eyes vacant and misty-looking, his hands shaking. Just like Dad's were.

I freeze, flattening my body to the wall behind a bookcase. As soon as Mr Cane looks away, I sprint down the corridor, round the corner and straight into Rusty.

He immediately starts babbling, "I was in maths, and you know I love maths, but we didn't do any maths... Mrs Hardgrave started writing a list of rules on the board..."

So he's finally noticing something's wrong. Good. He's also answered one of my seven thousand questions: whatever is going on isn't only happening to my class.

I grab his arm. "Mr Cane is locking all the doors. We need to get out of here."

7

We've just reached the exit to the playground when shoes squeak on the linoleum behind us.

I pull Rusty beneath the staircase and we both hunker down on our knees, watching through the slats in the stairs as Mr Cane rounds the corner.

He pauses beside the staircase, moustache twitching. I hold my breath.

He tilts his head to one side as though he's listening and then he's off, shuffling away down the corridor.

We don't discuss it; it's instinctive. The moment Mr Cane disappears, we both jump up and rush outside, racing across the playground, ash flying at our heels.

We're out of the gate, feet thumping down Coal

Road, when a small boy in old-fashioned clothing sprints across the street in front of us and disappears behind a lamp post.

I skid to a halt.

"Where did he go?"

Rusty shrugs. "I don't care about some kid. I just want to get home and figure out what's going on. School wasn't normal. Mr Cane and Mrs Hardgrave's hands were shaking. They looked dead behind the eyes too. A bit like Mrs Maudlin in the shop—"

A fire fizzes in my belly and I forget about the disappearing boy.

"Mrs Maudlin was acting weird? Why didn't you say anything earlier?"

"I just thought she had a cold."

I roll my eyes.

"You know I can't think on an empty stomach," he whines. "And Mrs Maudlin's hands always shake. It wasn't until I'd fully digested my wholesome snacks that I started to think about how she was even more juddery than normal. Then Jai didn't want to talk about the Battle Beast tournament. Then Mrs Hardgrave and her creepy list and croaky voice... I wanted to pretend everything was okay, but it's not, is it? What's going on?"

I wish I had the answer. I'm just praying Mum and Dad are back to normal. I really don't want to be figuring out what's going on with only Rusty for company.

We set off again, the wasteland looming off to the left. Beyond that, I can't see anything. All the ash in the air is blocking the view.

The basement, the urn and the ashes niggle away at me. I should tell Rusty. But I can't shake the feeling we're being watched even though the streets are empty. We cut down Lantern Lane and Rusty glances up at the windows of the tightly packed houses. He stops walking so suddenly I bash into him.

"Rusty!" I hiss.

"Look," he whispers.

Faces are pressed against the glass, not of just one or two windows, but all of them. Their expressions are strangely blank, and all eyes are focused on us.

"Why do I feel like we're standing out for all the wrong reasons?" whispers Rusty.

My heart is thumping. What is happening to everyone and why aren't we affected?

"What do you say to running the rest of the way home?"

Rusty doesn't argue, so we sprint.

*　　*　　*

Phrank welcomes us home in a flurry of brown feathers and sharp claws.

"Not now, Phrank!" I fend him off with one hand and fumble under the mat for the key with the other.

"Ow!" yells Rusty, as Phrank gets a peck in. "What's wrong with your flipping pheasant?"

Ever since Phrank got into the house through an open window and found his favourite treat of sunflower seeds, he's been desperate to sneak back inside.

I open the door.

"Don't let—" I begin and before I can finish with "the pheasant in" both Rusty and Phrank barge past me.

Phrank makes a beeline for the kitchen. There's a squawk of glee followed by the clatter of plates.

Mum and Dad would have kittens if they saw Phrank helping himself to our breakfast. I take in the messy plates and my anxiety spikes. They haven't cleared the table. Dad's a neat freak. He's all "a tidy house shows a tidy mind". This isn't right.

"Mum! Dad!" shouts Rusty.

There's no answer, which could still be a good sign. Maybe Mum's just busy with her studies and Dad is absorbed by yet another spreadsheet.

Rusty rushes off into the sitting room and the next thing I hear is a whimper.

I take a deep breath, preparing myself for the worst, and follow him in.

Mum and Dad are sitting on the green squishy sofa, straight-backed, hands on knees. They're staring at the TV as though they're watching their favourite programme, *Six Feet Under*.

The problem is there's nothing on the TV. The screen is blank.

I move round the sofa to stand in front of them, beside Rusty, and now it's my turn to whimper.

It's their eyes. They're way worse than Mr Cane's. They're like hard-boiled eggs – all white, no pupils. Why did that radio announcement tell us to carry on as normal when no one and nothing is normal? Well, apart from Rusty and me, but that doesn't make any sense either.

I swallow and it feels like I'm sucking on barbed wire.

Rusty's bottom lip is quivering. He grabs Dad's arm.

"Dad? Wake up."

Dad twitches once and then goes motionless.

Rusty drops Dad's arm and kneels beside Mum.

"Mum? It's me. What's wrong with you?" Rusty's voice is breaking, and he starts shaking Mum's legs, willing them to move.

Heart hammering, I wave my hands in front of Dad's face.

No reaction. It's like they are completely powered down. How have things gone from odd to downright scary so quickly? It's the stuff of horror movies and, to make matters worse, Rusty is making rank gulping noises. I think he might be about to cry.

This has gone too far.

"Stay here," I say. "I'm getting help."

I go out into the hallway and pick up the phone. I'm poised, ready to punch in the numbers 999, but there's no dial tone.

The landline is dead.

The muscles in my arms feel weak and it takes me a few goes to replace the handset. The lines must be down, but it's not a disaster yet. I run upstairs to get my mobile. I left it plugged in to charge, next to my bed. When it still won't turn on, panic, hot and sour-tasting, rises up my throat.

In the kitchen, Phrank is living his best life, polishing off toast crumbs and spilled cereal and bowls of milk. He looks up as though he's expecting me to tell him off. As soon as it becomes clear that I'm not going to do that, he takes it as his cue to dive head-first into a box of Wheatie Hoops.

At least one of us is having fun.

I open Dad's laptop. The screen stays blank, even when I try the on/off button about fifty times.

Goosebumps prickle my skin as though I've been dunked in ice, and I grip the edge of the kitchen counter.

We're cut off.

The bright pink radio is sitting innocently next to the toaster, at arm's length from the kitchen table.

I click it on.

"An ash cloud has settled on Greyscar after an incident at Oldcastle Steelworks. There is no cause for alarm. Continue your day as normal... An ash cloud—"

I fiddle with the tuner, but every channel is playing the same message.

I click it off.

Slowly, I walk back into the sitting room, more confused than ever; what am I going to say to Rusty? I don't know if it's because I'm older (I was born twenty-eight minutes before he was), but I've always been the more confident twin and even though he's a major pain in the bum, I feel kind of responsible for my "little" brother.

He looks up at me hopefully, but I don't meet his eyes. Instead, I stare out of the window where the ash has started to fall again in lacy grey flakes.

When I finally speak, the words feel heavy on my tongue.

"The phones are dead."

"What?" Rusty stands up, loosening his school tie and top button. "All of them?"

He takes out his mobile and stares at the stubbornly black display like he's willing it to magically turn on and connect. Then he begins stabbing at it. I shake my head.

"It won't work."

"Why?" says Rusty.

My mind is whirring desperately, trying to find an explanation. I don't want to say the words that are in my head. When I do, they catch in my throat like they don't want to come out.

"Nothing's working. I think we're on our own."

The words hang in the air like a bad smell.

"*Not quite*," says a voice from the hallway.

I freeze, body trembling. It can't be... It isn't possible...

"Grandpa?" I whisper.

8

Grandpa looks a bit fuzzy around the edges, but otherwise, he's just as I remember him: twinkly eyes, neatly combed quiff, blue suit trousers and a freshly ironed pink shirt.

"*Hello, Bug,*" he says, mouth breaking into a smile.

No one's called me that since he died. I don't think about the hows and whys; I run into his arms... and straight out the other side.

OMG, it's like running through freezing mist. My skin tingles and I wrap my arms around myself.

"You're...you're a—"

"*I think the word you're looking for is 'ghost'.*"

Part of our family has been missing since Grandpa died. I've longed to see him again, imagined what it might be like if I could talk to him one last time. But I never, not once, imagined him like this: all walk-through-able and cold as pond water. I take a step away from him.

His smile sags.

"I've been desperate to talk to you, but I could only make the lights flicker till now."

"That was you?" I say, thinking of all the times I've cursed bad electrics.

"That was me."

Rusty's wide-eyed and clutching the wall as though bracing himself. I'm frozen to the spot, but my brain is racing, trying to connect the dots to explain why we can see and hear him now. What's changed? And then the answer hits me.

"The urn," I whisper.

"What urn?" says Rusty.

Grandpa and I exchange a look.

"Will someone please tell me what's going on?" says Rusty, swaying slightly as though the shock of seeing Grandpa again has unbalanced him.

"Have you noticed your senses have been heightened since your twelfth birthday? You've been hearing things..."

I nod. I don't need a bat detector to hear bat calls and I'm certainly not enjoying having a bedroom next to the family bathroom.

73

I look at Rusty. He's nodding too.

"You've been seeing things too. People are there and then suddenly they aren't."

I think of the top-hatted men I saw from my window and who were gone in a blink of my eyes; the white figure I thought was Sadie but who vanished into the graveyard and the boy who disappeared behind the lamp post on Coal Road. I swallow.

"I meant to tell you when you turned twelve. I knew I had to. You both carry the mark."

He holds up his left arm to show the grey-blue fingerprint birthmark on his skin. It's the same as mine and Rusty's. I always knew it was something we shared, but I'm starting to get the feeling there's more to it than that.

"You said it meant I was good at maths," says Rusty, frowning.

A smile flits across Grandpa's face like the sun coming out from behind a cloud. *"You didn't need me to say you were good at maths. What you needed was for me not to die suddenly of a heart attack. What you needed was for me to tell you that mark is a ghost mark."*

I pull up my sleeve and rub at the strange grey-blue smudge on my arm. Rusty does the same.

"So, what does it mean exactly?" I hardly dare ask the question. I can tell it's not something warm and fluffy or

Grandpa would have mentioned it before.

"*It means you and your brother can see and communicate with the dead.*"

The mark looks like a fingerprint: a ghostly fingerprint. I shudder and there's a bang as Rusty's head hits the wall.

"What are you doing?" I hiss.

"Trying to wake up."

I pinch his arm hard.

"OW!"

"See," I say. "You're awake."

"Wish I blummin' wasn't," he grumbles, rubbing his arm.

"The ash...everyone acting weird...Mum and Dad..." I say. "Is it because of this ghost mark? Is it our fault?"

Grandpa shakes his head sadly.

"*If anyone is at fault, it's me. Let's discuss this over a cup of tea and some cake. You're going to need something sweet to help you digest this.*"

Back in the kitchen, I put the kettle on before cutting into an angel cake, rhythmically slicing through the bright pink and yellow layers. The vanilla filling perfumes the air, reminding me of the honeysuckle in the graveyard and calming my racing thoughts.

I push a slice of cake towards Rusty, the colour returning to his cheeks as he eats.

Grandpa takes a seat at the head of the table. He doesn't need to pull the chair out like a normal person, he just sort of floats into it. I can't stop staring at him. All I want is for him to give me a hug and tell me everything is going to be okay, but he can't do either. Everything isn't okay. We're in the middle of an ashy disaster and he's a ghost. When I look carefully, I can see all the way through him to the wooden chair behind.

It's the strangest thing to have a person you love both here and not here. I feel full and empty at the same time.

"My grandmother told me about the ghost mark when I was ten years old," begins Grandpa. *"I was too young. It was a burden I carried with me from that day on. I was relieved when your dad was born without it – he and your mum know nothing of its real meaning – but then I knew it could still pass to his children..."*

The kettle pings and I fill the teapot and put it on the table before taking a seat beside Rusty. I pour myself a large cup of tea and spoon in three sugars to calm my nerves.

Phrank pokes his head out of a cereal packet. We all ignore him. We've got bigger problems than a pheasant stealing breakfast.

"Go on," I say.

"Slowly," adds Rusty, rubbing his eyes. "I feel like I've woken up in a nightmare."

Grandpa leans forward in his chair and steeples his hands.

"The ghost mark can skip generations, but it is carried by our line of Smiths, or to use our full surname, Spooksmiths."

Rusty and I both drop our slice of cake at the same time.

"Back up," says Rusty. "You're telling us we don't even know our own name!"

"A wordsmith works with words. A blacksmith works with metal. A person who works with spirits is a Spooksmith."

This has gone far enough. Rusty's turned paler than an arctic hare and I'm sure I must look similar.

"We're supposed to work with spirits?" Rusty asks. "Like actually talk to ghosts?"

Grandpa nods.

"What if we don't want to?" I ask.

"It isn't a choice. It is a fact. A child born with the mark usually begins to manifest Spooksmith powers around their twelfth birthday."

I sink lower in my chair.

"I know it's a lot, but it's imperative that you understand the powers you have been given. In times of grave danger, your ability to see, hear and ward off ghosts is amplified. This is why you can

see and hear me now, and why you are unaffected by what is happening to the rest of the townsfolk."

"I don't get any of it," says Rusty. "What have our ghosty powers got to do with all the ash and Mum and Dad acting like zombies?"

"*Most ghosts do no harm, but for the ones that do, there is a secret crypt beneath our house—*"

"A what now?" Rusty's eyes look like they are about to pop out of his head. I look at the floor. I should have mentioned it to him earlier.

"*A crypt,*" continues Grandpa patiently. "*In it are urns containing the ashes of evil people who cannot be trusted to rest in peace. They are old, from a time when – for some unknown reason – dangerous ghosts kept coming back to terrorize Greyscar. We have never failed in our duty to keep these urns safe and secure. Until now.*"

Grandpa looks at me and I can't hold it in any longer.

"You might as well say it," I groan. "It's my fault, isn't it? Everything was fine until I found the crypt and dropped that urn."

"*I should have warned you.*" Grandpa's face softens. "*But the fact remains that a very dangerous ghost has been released.*"

I feel like a member of the Addams Family – a failed member, who's just made a deadly mistake.

78

By the look of him, Rusty feels even worse. He's just staring at me, too shocked to dole out his usual brotherly abuse.

"*He has covered Greyscar in his ashes, controlling everyone who inhales them.*"

"He?" I say, wrapping my hands around my tea, desperate to hold onto something warm and comforting and ordinary.

Grandpa gets up from the table, his feet not quite touching the floor. He drifts towards the boarded-up fireplace, deep in thought.

"*The urns are unmarked, the names of the deceased deliberately lost. It was thought that evil people were best forgotten because names have power. But I called this ghost 'he' because our town is covered in ashes. Or cinders...*"

The name from the nursery rhyme bubbles to the surface of my brain.

"The Cinderman," I say, a horrible queasy feeling fluttering deep in my belly. "You think the ghost taking over Greyscar is the Cinderman."

"The Cinderman?" splutters Rusty. "The bogeyman from that nursery rhyme? No way!"

"*There's one way for me to prove it to you, but you might not like it...*"

We follow Grandpa out of the kitchen and along the

79

hallway. Both Rusty and I turn our heads away from the sitting room as we pass it, trying not to see Mum and Dad sitting rigid in front of the blank television; trying not to feel the emptiness of life with zombie parents.

I'm glad when we're standing in front of the bookcase in the funeral parlour, and I have something else to focus on. I scan the tightly packed shelves, my mind a tangle of fears and questions.

"There's stuff about the Cinderman here?" I ask.

"*If a non-Spooksmith found a book with information like that...*" Grandpa shakes his head as if the thought is unimaginable. "*Spooksmiths pass on the knowledge verbally. It's an oral tradition: nothing is written down.*"

"Because that would make things waaay too easy," I grumble.

Grandpa ignores me and points at the bookcase. "*Remove the following books in the following places: second row from the top, six along; the first book in the bottom row; the seventh book in the fourth row and the ninth book along in the top row.*"

I pull the books out in the exact order he tells me, and the coffin-shaped door creaks open in the centre.

So, it's the position of the books not the books themselves that make the door open. I must have got lucky – or rather, unlucky – yesterday.

Rusty's mouth falls open. "I knew you were up to something last night. Why didn't you tell me our bookcase hid a Helldoor?"

I snort. "It's not a Helldoor. This isn't Battle Beast."

"Well, it's starting to feel a lot like it."

The cake obviously worked. My brother is back to being his obnoxious, Battle-Beast-obsessed self.

Grandpa directs me to a torch in the top drawer of his desk and motions for us to step through the door.

"After you," says Rusty.

"*I don't need a door,*" says Grandpa, disappearing through the shelves.

"Show off," I mutter, climbing through the doorway, Rusty behind me.

As soon as we step inside, the whispering noise returns, a chuntering nonsense filling the air.

I try to ignore it and flick the torch on.

I follow the stairs down. There's a hole in the wall to my right and a brown spider darts into it. It's a cave spider, I think. They're rarely spotted because they choose to live in total darkness. Any other time I'd be excited, but my attention is taken up with the whispering and the uneven stairs. Shallow grooves have been worn into the stone by all the feet that have come before me: Spooksmiths' feet.

I shiver. I'm literally walking in the footsteps of my ancestors. It seems there's no escaping the family business after all.

At the bottom of the stairs the temperature drops. I have to concentrate hard to stop my teeth chattering. We are standing in a low room with a vaulted ceiling. The beam from my torch doesn't reach the back of the room, so I have no idea how far it stretches, but a weird symbol is scratched into the wall on my left. It's a circle containing a triangle with the letters V.S., M.I. and L.W. at each point.

"It's like the insignia for Coven Devious," whispers Rusty.

"Stop it with the Battle Beast names," I hiss.

I haven't got time to work out what it is. I face the torch down and inwards.

A few paces in sits a long trestle table with urns spread along it. There must be over a hundred, some as small as Dad's espresso cup, others as tall as a large milk carton. They are all dull metal and covered in dust and matted cobwebs. As my torchlight passes over them, the whispering noise turns to calls and jeers.

A finger of dread crawls up my spine and I turn to face Grandpa.

"The urns...they're talking..."

"*Listen*," he urges.

There's a horde of screeching voices, so it takes me a moment to pick out individuals.

I don't like what I hear.

"Free us like you freed the Cinderman!"

"You will pay for your crimes!"

"We are coming for you!"

Cackles and cries swirl around me. I clamp my hands over my ears and bolt for the stairs.

9

Phrank is fast asleep beside the still-warm kettle when Rusty and I burst into the kitchen. He lets out an ear-splitting squawk of fury at being disturbed and another one as Grandpa shoots through the door after us.

"As long as the lids remain shut, I can assure you those urns are perfectly safe—"

"Perfectly safe!" I splutter. "I've just been threatened by a crypt of crazed killers!"

"*I* was there too, you puffed-up princess," says Rusty.

"Who are you calling a 'puffed-up princess'? You garbage-loving chaos goblin."

"*Enough!*" shouts Grandpa.

We both jump. I've never heard him yell before, but I can tell he's angry. He's got little wisps of ghostly mist drifting off him like steam.

"*I've spent too long listening to you two fighting. When are you going to realize that you need each other?*"

Huffily, I pull out a chair at the table, and sit down.

Rusty does the same.

It's been a long time since we've needed anything from each other. From the way Rusty is glaring at me through the cereal packets, I'd say he's thinking the same thing.

"*I was alone with the ghost mark. You are lucky. There are two of you: a team.*"

Grandpa might have a point. Whoever this Cinderman is, I don't want to face him alone.

"Sorry," I say.

"Sorry too," Rusty says. Then he smirks and flicks a Wheatie Hoop at me. "Garbage-loving chaos goblin was one of your finer put-downs."

I grin back at him.

Grandpa takes his seat at the head of the table.

"*We need a plan. It's only eight hours until sunset.*"

"Hang on," I say. "There's a deadline?"

I thought things couldn't get much worse, but it turns out they can.

"It's always just before sunset. Or sunrise. Or midnight," says Rusty. "It depends on the evil force you are battling, but they're the times of day when the barrier between the living and the dead is at its thinnest and the forces of darkness are at their peak."

"And you know this because…?"

"Battle Beast."

"Obviously." I look pleadingly at Grandpa, hoping he's going to tell me Rusty's talking rubbish.

"Rusty is correct. I don't know about Battle Beast, but when dealing with ghosts, my grandmother told me that sunset is the deadline. Until that moment an escaped ghost can be stopped and everyone under their control can be saved. After that moment, the Cinderman will be too strong. Who knows where he will stop?"

I sink my head into my hands. "Why is he doing this?"

"When you dropped the urn, he said something, didn't he?"

I nod miserably. If only I'd kept my nerve and not thrown the urn away.

"He said, 'Speak my name.'" I pause. "I think he wants to be remembered."

Grandpa presses his hands into the table. His fingers actually disappear into the wood.

"Then he must be wiped from history. A person's real name has power. It must still be in books, letters, objects he cared for. It is your job to find and destroy all mentions of his name. It must be the thing that is giving him a foothold in the living world.

Hopefully, that will weaken him enough for you to defeat him."

"Hopefully?" I splutter. "You don't sound too sure."

"My knowledge is limited to what my grandmother told me. No one has ever freed a ghost from one of the crypt's urns before—"

"Hang on," interrupts Rusty. "Just to be clear, we are the only ones with the powers to stop this?"

Grandpa nods his head.

"What about the symbol in the crypt?" I ask, unable to keep the desperation out of my voice. "Maybe those letters around the triangle are initials. Could they mean that other families have powers too? Could they help?"

"To my knowledge, our line of Smiths are the only ones with the ghost mark," says Grandpa. *"Besides, Greyscar is cut off from the outside world by the Cinderman's ash haze. No one can get in and no one can get out."*

"Great," I say. "Rusty and I are the team standing between Greyscar and never-ending ash monster domination."

"And Phrank," adds Grandpa with a smile.

"Phrank?" I splutter.

"Spooksmiths often have an animal sidekick."

Phrank waddles across the counter and starts clawing at the bread bin. A Wheatie Hoop is stuck around one of his claws like an edible bangle.

"You're telling me that fleabag is our sidekick?" Rusty points at Phrank.

"*More usually it's a cat or a dog, but as all the other animals have left and you seem to have a bond with this pheasant...*"

Rusty lets out a hysterical laugh. One is bubbling up inside me too. I look at Phrank. He's given up on the bread bin and has settled back down beside the kettle to groom himself. I love him, but how much help can a pheasant be?

"*The important point is that you are not alone,*" says Grandpa. "*You have each other, Phrank and me. Plus, there are ghosts all over Greyscar who may know something and be persuaded to help.*"

It turns out Miss Chen was onto something with her ghost tours after all. I shake my head. This would blow Dad's mind. If he wasn't a zombie... Tears well up at the thought of my parents under the control of some evil ghost, but I blink them away. Crying won't help them.

"I think we hit the graveyard," says Rusty.

"*Excellent choice,*" says Grandpa. "*Little Hope Graveyard is a favourite meeting place for the stronger category of ghost. Not that I've ever been as a ghost...*"

"Why not?" I ask.

"*Category One Ghosts, like me, can't leave the place they died. I am tied to this house.*"

"But you were a Spooksmith, how come you're only Category One?" I can't believe he isn't more powerful in death – I really want him to come with us. "And what's with this weird rating system?"

"*Spooksmiths categorize ghosts to gauge their potential for trouble. A more angry person often becomes a higher category and more powerful ghost.*"

"I get it," says Rusty. "Standard bad-guy ranking."

Of course *he* gets it, Battle Beasters are obsessed with stats, but something is troubling me.

"Are we going to be meeting a lot of angry ghosts in the graveyard then?" I ask.

"*Your Category Twos and Threes are generally all right,*" explains Grandpa. "*It's your Fours and Fives you've got to watch out for, but most of them are locked in our crypt.*"

Most of them are. Except for the one that I let go. I shift my feet.

"Does everyone who dies become a ghost?" asks Rusty quietly.

"*No,*" says Grandpa with a shake of his head. "*Most move on to whatever lies beyond, but some of us get stuck. Category Ones – like myself – are the most common. We've lived good lives and been – more or less – good people, but we have unfinished business. I'd failed to tell you about the mark and your powers.*"

I'm relieved Grandpa stuck around – we'd be in serious trouble without him – but I feel bad he's been here for the past three months and unable to communicate. His lack of ghostly powers must be very frustrating and he looks pained that he can't help us more. I want to look after him for a change.

"You stay here and watch over Mum and Dad. I guess we're Spooksmiths now. We've got this, right?" I wish I sounded more confident.

"Yeah," says Rusty, following my lead. "I think I can handle grilling graveyard ghosts for info."

"*Remember, your Spooksmith skills protect you against a ghost's influence, but they don't make you invincible. The Cinderman is a powerful ghost. A Category Five – a true horror. Which is why you need some weapons.*"

"Weapons?" says Rusty. He's got that mad glint in his eye. I've seen it when he's gaming. Or thinking about gaming. "Now you're talking. What did you have in mind?"

"*Salt.*"

Rusty doesn't even blink at this ridiculous suggestion.

"What?" I say, unable to believe that he's serious.

"*Salt is a well-known defence against ghosts—*"

"It's like Battle Beast: Return of the Lurkers," Rusty takes over.

I groan, but he's obviously determined to tell the full story.

"I had twenty-four hours to hit Kralex's check point, sneak through the Desert of Souls and kill Zendar before Jai's team of ghostly Griefers took me out. It took nine of my Beast Dwellers' lives to gather enough salt tokens, but it was my most successful weapon."

He grabs the salt mill, frowning to find it empty. He tosses it back and shoots out of the room and up the stairs before I can question him.

"Do you know where Mum keeps those fancy, salty bath bombs?" he yells from the landing.

"We're trying to take down the Cinderman, not organizing a spa night!" I shout back.

I look to Grandpa to be the sensible one, but he's got that proud look on his face like he actually agrees with whatever nonsense Rusty is up to.

Grandpa points to a packet of sage and onion stuffing sitting on the kitchen counter.

"*Sage is delicious with sausages and chicken and it's another powerful ghost deterrent. Along with lavender.*" His head literally disappears into the spice cupboard. "*Which we don't appear to have any of...*"

I groan. I know where there's some lavender. What's that

saying? *If you can't beat them, join them.* I head out of the kitchen and into the downstairs loo beneath the stairs. Sitting beside the toilet brush are two large cans of lavender-scented air freshener.

"Will this do?" I ask, emerging with the cans of Smell Fresh.

"Perfect!" declares Rusty, bounding down the stairs.

We go into the kitchen and Rusty shares the salt bombs between two rucksacks before adding a can of Smell Fresh to each. I can't believe our ghostbusting kit will be deadly for anything other than dirt and bad smells. I hand him the sage and onion stuffing.

"Forgot about sage. Good catch," he says, tucking the packet into the rucksack.

"How do you know all this?" I ask my brother.

"All elite Battle Beast gamers know salt, sage and lavender burn ghosts," says Rusty.

I have a million and one questions, but I expect the answers will make as much sense as using deodorizing spray on a ghost.

"Let's get this over with," I say, shouldering my rucksack.

"Oh, come on, Indigo, where's the enthusiasm?" asks Rusty. "What could be more fun than interviewing ghosts in a graveyard so we can learn how to wipe an ash-wielding ghost-monster from history?"

I'm glad he can make a joke of it. Maybe all those hours spent playing Battle Beast have prepared him for our new deadly reality.

"*Positive mental attitude, Bug,*" says Grandpa. "*It's never too late to turn things around.*"

I really hope he's right.

10

Little Hope Graveyard clings to the top of Greyscar cliffs like a drowning swimmer to a float. It knows its position is risky, that most of the church and several graves have already slid beneath the waves, but it hangs on.

I can't believe I was here less than twenty-four hours ago watching bats while Dad chatted to the Rev. Even though I'm not supposed to come here because of something called "subsidence", this is my happy place. The graveyard is usually full of wildlife and on a clear day you can see all the way to Wreck Island, an amazing sanctuary for birds. Today though, the wildlife has gone and an ashy fog blocks my view. I feel like I'm trapped inside a nightmarish snow globe.

Rusty and I hover by the gate, the wind whipping up the ash and setting the lantern in the metal entrance arch swinging. It creaks above our heads. I can't shake the feeling it's telling us to turn back.

"It's like the end of the world," I shout over the wind.

"Ashmageddon," Rusty shouts back, the tails of his long blue coat billowing around him. He thinks it makes him look like some character from Battle Beast. I think he looks like a wannabe Batman.

I frown.

"Like Armageddon," he adds, "but with more ash."

Despite everything, I smile. He has a way with words. Not that I'd ever tell him.

We push on, into the graveyard. I'm struggling to get my bearings in all the ash, when a vibration in the air sends goosebumps rippling down my arms.

"Did you hear that?" I shout to Rusty.

"Yup," he replies, although he looks like he wishes he hadn't.

We follow the hum rising from the ground like a swarm of locusts.

The wind is pelting us with pieces of bone-sharp ash, as though it's trying to drive us away. I can't see my hand in front of my face, but as I move through the graveyard the hum gets louder until I can pick out voices and the sound of laughter.

Rusty reaches for my hand. I take it. It's damp with sweat and if I wasn't so scared, I'd have immediately shaken him off.

"I think the voices are coming from over—"

I don't get to finish my sentence. The ground at our feet crumbles into nothing. It turns out Dad was right to warn me, and I just have time to think the word *sinkhole* before we're falling.

The voices cut out as we drop through the earth in a screaming ball of arms and legs. Rusty is making a high-pitched squealing sound. It's the sort of noise a pig might make if it did a bungee jump.

My stomach lurches as we land on a pile of soft and squelchy seaweed. Rusty abruptly stops squealing and I make an involuntary *huff* sound as the air is knocked from my lungs.

Slimy strands of seaweed slip through my fingers as I sit up, inhaling the scent of salty, rotting vegetation.

Light creeps in from the hole we fell through and from a larger opening in the cliff, about two bus lengths ahead of us.

I can make out rocky walls, crumbling stone pillars...and eight stone coffins.

"Rusty!" I shake his shoulder excitedly. "We're in Little Hope Crypt."

The irony is not lost on me. I'd never have thought in a

million years I'd be happy to find myself in a burial vault. What a difference a day makes.

"Are we dead?" says Rusty, groaning and rolling over.

A burst of childish ghostly chuckling sounds from nearby and I shiver.

"Who's there?" I ask, spinning around, heart thumping.

A see-through toddler sporting blond curls and a sailor suit pops out of the sarcophagus in front of me.

"*Boo!*" says the toddler.

I scream and Rusty falls off the mound of seaweed.

The toddler points and cackles at us so hard he has to clasp his transparent sides.

By the time I've recovered my cool – and Rusty's got up off the floor – the toddler is sitting cross-legged on top of a stone coffin.

"*Fluffy and bouncy.*" He speaks with a lisp, pointing at our hair and then at his own, jiggling up and down with excitement.

"This kid gives me the creeps," whispers Rusty, sidling up to me.

"Be nice," I hiss, before turning to the excitable tot. "Is there a grown-up around that we can speak to?"

The child howls with laughter and Rusty and I exchange a glance. It's a few seconds before the kid manages to control himself enough to talk, accompanied by the occasional mirth-filled snort.

"*Chuckles over a hundred years old!*"

I freeze. I know that name.

"Chuckles?" whispers Rusty, not even trying to hide the disbelief in his voice. "Chuckles the Phantom Toddler who Miss Chen's always going on about?"

I'm starting to wish I'd taken one of her tours.

"*Chuckles famous!*" he cackles.

I can see how he got his nickname, but he could just as easily have been called "Irritating Infant" or "Pain In The Bum". Not that I point this out. We're here to get information on the Cinderman, so we need Chuckles's help.

"Hi there, Chuckles, I'm Indigo and this is Rusty—"

"*Chuckles knows who you are,*" he giggles, "*and he can guess why you're here. We all can.*"

"We?" I ask hopefully. Please let there be another more sensible ghost to talk to. Preferably one that doesn't keep referring to themselves in third person...

"*Others are here. They're hiding because they don't want to talk to you.*"

Oh.

"Why not?" asks Rusty, stepping out from behind me.

"*Why? The Cinderman*" – Chuckles whispers the name

before loudly continuing – "*can control live humans and ghosts. They are scared.*"

I swallow. If other ghosts are frightened of the Cinderman, what chance do Rusty and I have?

"But *you're* talking to us," I say.

"*Chuckles enjoys company. And talking. And laughing.*"

He reaches out to pet Rusty's curls and Rusty bats him away, his hand passing straight through Chuckles's head.

Chuckles pouts and reaches up his arms.

"*Carry!*"

"No way," says Rusty.

I'm not so quick to give up. I'm thinking if we humour this tiny terror, we might start getting some answers.

"He wants you to pick him up." I glare at Rusty.

"*You* pick him up."

"*Carry! Carry! Carry!*" Chuckles cries, stretching his ghostly arms towards Rusty.

Rusty grimaces.

I turn my back on Chuckles and push my face close to Rusty's, trying not to inhale his stinky tweenage boy smell.

"He wants *you* and we need to ask him some questions, so be nice and play along."

I feel like a mother encouraging her kid on an unpopular playdate.

"You owe me," Rusty hisses, opening his arms to Chuckles.

Chuckles leaps into them, somehow wrapping his chunky-looking yet see-through legs around Rusty's middle. I don't understand the ghost mechanics behind it, but Chuckles is obviously the kind of ghost who is able to make himself just solid enough to hold on.

"Ergh," says Rusty. "It's like being hugged by a wet cloud."

"Rusty..." I warn him, before turning to Chuckles. "What do you know about the Cinderman?"

I've said the name full-volume, and in response, wailing starts up from the sea. It's like a scream mixed with a squeaking door. If you've ever heard a barn owl in full squawk, it's similar, only louder and more piercing.

"What is that?" says Rusty, staring at the opening in the cliff.

I shake my head. "I don't know and I'm not sure I want to find out."

Chuckles is giggling like he's found his favourite cuddly toy, but whatever is making that noise sounds about as cuddly as a werewolf.

And it's getting closer.

11

The screaming stops and a shimmering shape swims through the opening in the cliff above the sea. It's a woman in a long white gown, streaked with seaweed and slime. She drifts towards us, long black hair hanging limp either side of her face, mouth stretched into a silent scream.

The sight of her makes my attempt at ghost etiquette run for the hills and I flinch. Even in my worst nightmares I've never seen a face so tormented. Rusty doesn't appear to be a fan of this ghost either. He seems to be trying to use Chuckles as a sort of shield, cowering behind him as though he was a solid object. Not that this seems to worry Chuckles, who is grinning from ear to ear.

"*Banshee!*" he cries.

"The Blasted Banshee?" I say, thinking back to last night when Sadie was desperate to tell her story.

"The one who dived into a flooded mine to find her daughter only for them both to drown and now haunts the coast with her screams – that Banshee?"

Chuckles nods and Banshee lifts her black eyes towards mine. They're twin pits of despair and I reel backwards, hit by an overwhelming sense of sorrow.

"There is truth buried in stories," she whispers. *"You just have to dig deep enough to find it."* Her voice is low and slow. It's the kind of voice that sounds as though it knows secrets: deep, dark secrets that will turn hair white with fright.

I gulp.

"We're looking for information about the Cinderman. Can you help us?"

Banshee shakes her head slowly, her long hair swaying like seaweed in a current.

"I will not."

The muscles in Rusty's face tense.

"He's destroying the town and hurting our parents and friends!"

"Speak of the devil and you give him power."

Frustrated, I kick out at the stone coffin in front of me, hurting my toes and chipping the bottom corner, sending a chunk of limestone skittering across the floor.

"Temper, temper," chuckles Chuckles.

I ignore him, which is easier for me than for Rusty when Chuckles is clinging limpet-like around his neck.

"If you won't help us, why are you here?" I ask.

"*I'm here to tell you to stop.*"

"Stop?" says Rusty, wrestling with Chuckles, who is trying to straddle his shoulders.

"*That abomination taking over your town makes cinders of anyone in his path. That is how he got his name. My advice is to try to use your powers to break through the ghost fog and escape, while you still can.*"

This Banshee character really is a piece of work.

"Leave?" I say, a furious heat flooding my chest. "Abandon our parents and our friends? Just hand Greyscar over without a fight?"

"*It is hopeless. I should know.*"

"What do you know?" I urge, hoping that the woman this ghost once was is still there, hiding behind this frankly terrifying exterior. "Who were you?"

"*I used to be Etta Hyde. I knew a fearless girl like you… I could not save her…*" Banshee trails off, shaking her head. The way she says it makes it sound like they were close. I take a guess.

"Your daughter?" I ask.

"*My daughter, Ivy. She is lost, drowned in Greyscar Mine, and however hard I search I cannot find her. Even in death…*"

She turns her back and drifts towards the sea making a faint moaning sound and trailing tendrils of ghostly mist.

I can't let her leave.

"I'm sorry about Ivy," I shout after her. "But we came here for answers and if we don't get them Rusty and I will lose our family like you lost Ivy."

She ignores me, continuing to drift away, moaning. I pick up the piece of stone I chipped off the coffin and hurl it at her back. It sails straight through her, hitting the opposite wall with a tinny chink.

"Instead of all the crying and wailing, why don't you do something?" I yell.

"*If he is here, it is already too late to save the ones you love,*" she says, continuing to float away and taking the moaning up an octave.

"It's never too late to turn things around!" I repeat Grandpa's advice to me, my voice echoing around the crypt.

Banshee pauses and for a moment I think she might be about to reconsider.

"*Goodbye, Indigo Spooksmith,*" she says. Then she steps through the crypt wall and disappears.

"Fine!" I yell. "Be like that! We'll find another ghost to help us!"

The rocky walls around us start to whisper, but no other spirit steps forward.

"Er, Indigo…" says Rusty, clinging to Chuckles. "I don't think they sound happy to help."

But I'm not stopping. In fact, I'm just getting started. How dare all these wimpy phantoms do nothing?

"I know you're all there, watching. You should be ashamed of yourselves. There must be hundreds of you and there's only one Cinderman."

At the mention of his name the whispering gets louder, and I realize something, something born from years of perseverance staking out bogs looking for grass snakes and walking endless trails hoping for a red squirrel sighting. That if you keep going, keep pushing even when it seems you're getting nowhere, you can accomplish anything.

I start to chant, "Cinderman. Cinderman. Cinder—"

A shaven-headed ghost with a monocle drifts out from behind the closest tomb.

"You should be careful. You might get what you wish for."

Another ghost appears behind the monocled one; this one wears an orange turban with gold-rimmed glasses suspended from his neck.

"Bernard," says the turbaned ghost. *"They're only children."*

Chuckles giggles. *"Let Chuckles introduce you to the*

librarians, Bernard and Tanvir."

"Well, I'm Indigo and I want to destroy the Cinderman. We need a name. Will you help me?"

There's a load more ghostly whispering during which Rusty takes a jammy biscuit out of his pocket and starts nervously crunching it.

Chuckles also takes one. He *tries* to eat it, but every bite just falls through him to the floor.

"*I don't think it's a good idea to tell them about the letters,*" I overhear Tanvir whisper.

"What letters?" I ask.

Bernard ignores me and continues talking to Tanvir.

"*You don't get a say in this—*"

"*That is out of order,*" says Tanvir. "*I was Head Librarian after you, so by rights I should get more of a say.*"

"*Oh, shut your big mouth—*"

"*We've talked about your very personal attacks before and I will not stand for it.*"

All this bickering is getting ridiculous. I can see how it winds Mum and Dad up when Rusty and I do it.

"Please just tell us what you know and we'll stop bothering you," I say.

"*The real name of the ghost taking over this town is said to be mentioned in some private correspondence,*" says Bernard.

"And where would we find that?" I ask.

"Greyscar House," says Bernard, smiling nastily.

"But the house has fallen into the mine," Rusty says.

"Nonsense," says Bernard, with a scoff.

"Bernard, stop this!" protests Tanvir.

Bernard doesn't listen. *"The house's position is precarious, but it's still there. The letters are said to be kept in a bureau or desk. If only someone could go there and look—"*

"You know as well as I that the mining tunnels beneath Greyscar House make it too dangerous and unstable for anyone to visit," says Tanvir.

"If we go, we could end up under the Cinderman's control," snaps Bernard. *"She released him. She must do her part."*

I swallow. Bernard's right. I started this. I look at Rusty, who is still stuck with Chuckles.

"I can go on my own—"

"No way," says Rusty. "If you go, I go."

I think that's the nicest thing he's ever said to me, but Chuckles has no intention of losing his new BFF.

"No. No. No!" says Chuckles. He sticks his thumb in his mouth and wraps his legs more tightly around Rusty's waist.

"This is important, Chuckles," says Rusty. "I have to get these letters. My grandpa told me names have power and that if my sister and I can destroy all mentions of the

Cinderman's real name then we can somehow defeat him and get our parents and our town back. I'm not sure it will work, but you have to let me try."

I must admit that was a pretty good speech. It obviously worked on Chuckles because he gives Rusty an ectoplasmic kiss goodbye. Rusty even waits until Chuckles has returned to his coffin before wiping it off. If that's not a sign of personal growth, I don't know what is.

There's no time to waste. We climb up the cliff, back to the graveyard. The air smells of a thousand bonfires until we pass the grave with the vanilla-scented honeysuckle. I wonder whose grave it is and if he or she was watching in the crypt just now. Either way, the scent of the flowers is so much nicer than the smoky air. I break off a stem, stuffing the white petals down inside my coat so I can keep its comforting smell with me for longer.

The ash has risen since we've been in the crypt – now it's up to my calves – and it's eerily quiet. It's like being on an alien planet. There are no birds in the sky; no foxes sneaking along hedgerows or bats stirring from the belfry either. Anything that could escape already has.

The time is a mystery too. The twilight sky is no help because it's looked the same all day. And then I think of something.

"Rusty, what time do you think it is?"

Rusty stops walking and puts his hand on his belly.

"From my concave stomach and the rumblings within, I'd say it's somewhere around midday."

If he's right and it is around twelve, it's roughly seven hours before sunset. I exhale. Seven hours to defeat the Cinderman.

He takes two biscuits out of his rucksack and hands one to me.

"Thanks," I say.

I focus on the crunch of my biscuit rather than on the unsettling crunch of my feet in the ash as we walk towards Greyscar House.

Does the Cinderman know we're here? Can he sense us? See us? I speed up, uncomfortably aware of the trail of footprints we're leaving behind.

As we turn on to Bat Lane a flash of red catches my eye.

Two kids wearing Saltburn Academy jumpers are creeping through the ash towards us.

With a shudder, I recognize them: Sadie...and Dexter.

Except it's not really Sadie and Dexter. Their movements are jerky; their smiles false. I have a feeling that fun and friendship are the last things on their mind...

12

"Rusty," I hiss. "We've got company."

"Is it me, or do Dexter and Sadie look really messed up?" he says.

I take in Dexter's ripped jumper and scruffy hair and I instantly get the jitters. He's the kind of person who gels his hair and puts on a fresh T-shirt just to walk to the shops. Something tells me he's not the boy I bonded with over Captain Carrot right now.

We shrink back into a doorway and for a moment I think they're going to pass us by; then they turn to face us. I gasp. Their eyes are like boiled eggs – no pupils, just like Mum and Dad's.

"Can they see us?" asks Rusty.

I give a tentative wave.

Sadie steps forward. Her usually open and friendly face is twisted, her mouth curved in a crocodile smile.

My heartbeat quickens. They can see us all right. I feel scared – not just for me and Rusty, but for Sadie and Dexter too. What has the Cinderman done to them?

"You two have led us a merry dance." Her words are old-fashioned, and her voice choked, as though she's got a throat full of ash.

I take a shaky breath, suddenly very aware that they're blocking our exit. I wish Rusty and I had made a run for it when we had the chance.

"I'm sorry about the other night—"

Sadie cuts me off. "I tracked your footprints."

I freeze. I know that voice. It's the one that crackled over the radio. The same one Ms Vago and all the other teachers used.

"She sounds angry," Rusty whispers unhelpfully in my ear.

I ignore him.

"What do you want?" I try to keep my tone casual, but the words feel sticky in my mouth.

"You're a Spooksmith. We don't approve of Spooksmiths." Sadie winks a pupil-less eye at Dexter. He just keeps staring straight through me and Rusty like we're windows.

"Dexter?" I step forwards, reaching out and touching his shoulder.

He flinches, his white eyes swivelling from side to side.

They remind me of rolling balls on a pool table.

"Dexter, can you hear me?"

"Indigo?" He frowns, a tear trickling down his cheek with the effort to be himself. "Is that you?"

It's Dexter. It's his voice. I wrap my arms around him, so relieved to know my friend is still in there.

"Run," he whispers in my ear, before pushing me away.

"Wait—"

Dexter's face snaps back to vacant, like he's a puppet and the Cinderman has just picked up the strings.

I lock eyes with Rusty. He gives a single nod and together we rush them. Rusty rams Dexter, knocking him over like a skittle, and I barge past Sadie. It doesn't feel good. I don't want to leave Dexter or Sadie under the Cinderman's control, but what choice do I have?

We don't have time to discuss a plan, but there's no way I'm heading to Greyscar House and giving away our only lead if Dexter and Sadie are following us.

"Power of Harknock!" says Rusty, leaping over a partially buried dustbin lid, the tails of his coat flying out behind him.

What is he on about?

"Spawn Swipe," he says, skidding around a pile of boxes.

OMG, these are his gaming moves. He's pretending he's playing Battle Beast.

I'm about to hiss at him to shut up, when I notice that his commentary is making him move faster. It's so effective, I'm thinking about making up my own wacky gaming phrases. Then Sadie's ash-choked voice drifts towards us: "Come out, come out, wherever you are!"

I've got no idea how, but it sounds like she's ahead of us.

We're on Lantern Lane, surrounded by terraced houses. There's nowhere to hide.

I try the nearest door.

Locked.

And the next one.

And the next.

In desperation, I scan the street.

"There!" I shout, heart leaping as I spot a gap between number thirteen's door and the frame.

I run, ducking beneath an empty hanging basket, and push on the chipped red door with the hand-shaped knocker.

The door swings open, and I hurry inside.

Rusty follows, shutting the door behind us.

There's no key to lock it so I slip the safety chain across. It rattles loudly in the quiet.

We're in a hallway, surrounded by skull-patterned wallpaper and some sort of plastic flooring that squeaks when you step on it. There's the tang of woody incense but no sign of anyone.

I make for the stairs. Rusty shakes his head.

"If we get cornered up there, there's no way out."

He's good at strategy. I can't believe I'm thinking it, but thank you again, Battle Beast.

We creep into the front room.

Even though it's small, it's filled to bursting with dark wood furniture, ghost figurines and freaky-looking china dolls. Dreamcatchers hang from the ceiling and a mug saying *If you've got it, haunt it* sits on the coffee table in the centre. There's a map showing a bird's-eye view of Greyscar hanging on one wall. It's covered in little red dots, as though marking places of interest. One of the places with a pin through it is Serenity Funerals. Weird. My eyes skim over it, drawn to the collection of book-sized paintings hanging above the gas fire.

Most of them show crumbling mansions or towers, spooky-looking places with dark and stormy skies. The one that catches my eye though is different. It shows a girl about my age with flowing blond hair and an ankle-length white dress. She's holding a bunch of white flowers which twist out of the bouquet and up her arms, like honeysuckle climbing a wall. She stares out at me with bright blue, knowing eyes. There's something about her that looks familiar...

"Indigo," whispers Rusty, tugging on my sleeve.

I turn around, irritated to have been interrupted, and gasp.

In all the clutter, I missed the woman sitting behind me. She's on a dining chair wedged between a bookshelf and an upright piano.

I blink.

It's Miss Chen, the Creep It Real owner. She's in her signature purple tie-dye top and black leather skirt, gold hoop earrings dangling from her ears. I had no idea this was where she lived. I've only ever seen her in her booth or out on tours.

"Do you think she knows we're here?" whispers Rusty.

I shake my head, unsure. She seems to be powered down like Mum and Dad, but after seeing how fast Dexter and Sadie moved, I can't swear to it.

"Keep an eye on her while I check the street. If she so much as twitches, we're gone."

Even with Rusty standing guard, my shoulders tense as I turn my back on Miss Chen. I can't stop thinking about those stone angels in *Doctor Who*, who creep up on you the moment you look away. It's Dexter's favourite episode. I'd give anything to be sat watching it with him now.

A lacy net curtain hangs at the window. I kneel so my face

is level with the windowsill and lift the corner of the curtain a few centimetres.

Sadie sprints past the window, a flash of red and grey, followed by Dexter. They're fast. Really fast. It must be something to do with the Cinderman because they're moving at an unnatural speed. Hand shaking, I drop the curtain.

"Indigo," whispers Rusty.

"Shh," I hiss. "They're right outside."

"Indigo!" Rusty's voice has an urgent edge to it.

I turn around.

Miss Chen is standing up, right arm raised, index finger pointing straight at me.

13

"Let's get out of here." I'm pushing Rusty towards the door, when, *bang*, two hands hit Miss Chen's front window.

Both Rusty and I jump as Sadie's face pushes up against the glass, warped and featureless through the net curtain.

We freeze and she disappears again. For a moment, I let myself think she might not have seen us. Then I hear the creak of the front door handle followed by a loud *thunk*.

It's the sound of the door catching on the chain and it jolts me into action.

Miss Chen blinks, lowering her hand as we tear out of the room into the hallway. It's as though the Cinderman can't quite muster the power to control her fully as well as animate Sadie and Dexter.

There's no sign of Sadie now, but Dexter's got the front door open as wide as it will go, his arm reaching through the gap to unhook the chain.

Stopping him would involve hurting him. I hesitate, but Rusty doesn't. He rams the door with his shoulder. It slams onto Dexter's arm. Dexter doesn't make a sound – it's like he can't feel it – but he does pull his arm back.

It's all we need. I kick the door shut and Rusty drags the hall table behind it to form a flimsy barricade.

"It won't hold them for ever," he says.

As if I need reminding.

We dash through the kitchen, past a cup of cold jasmine tea and a greying pile of chopped vegetables, and out the back door. Miss Chen has a small courtyard garden, the same as all the other houses on the street. We cross it in three strides, vaulting the low gate and landing in the alleyway that runs along the back of the row of houses.

A crash and thump of footsteps behind tells us that Dexter has broken through the barricade.

Panic fires and adrenaline shoots through my veins. We tear down the alley, dodging dustbins, a broken football goal and a collapsed climbing frame, until we see Sadie.

She's standing at the entrance to Coal Road beside one of those big green recycling bins. She's got her back to us, so she hasn't seen us yet. It doesn't change the fact that we have to get round her.

We skid to a halt.

"What's she doing?" whispers Rusty.

"I don't know, but I say we charge her on three."

There's a crash behind as Miss Chen's gate is thrown open.

"Three!" Rusty shouts.

We charge.

Sadie spins around, lunging at us from the front at the same time as Dexter snatches wildly from behind.

"Zigzag!" shouts Rusty.

It's how we used to escape bathtime as little kids. I was always zig – dart right first –and Rusty was always zag – dart left first. It used to drive Mum and Dad bananas.

I lurch right then quickly left and Rusty does the opposite. But Dexter is moving too fast to slow down and Sadie's lunge has left her unbalanced. There's a howl of fury as the two collide, falling in a tangle of arms and legs, followed by silence.

Glancing back over my shoulder, I see Sadie and Dexter have frozen where they fell, like they've expended their usefulness. Was the Cinderman using them to find out something, or were they simply herding us? Either way, the only way to truly help them – to help everyone – is to find the

Cinderman's real name and stop him. So I run on, feet flying through the ash. It floats up, clouding the air, but we don't slow down until we cross a deserted Coal Road and reach the gates to Greyscar House and the mine.

Chains as thick as a man's arm are wrapped around the gates and *DANGER! KEEP OUT!* signs are strung along vicious, spike-topped railings.

But it's not the chains or spikes or signs that keep people out. It's the stories. The ones about sinkholes. And hidden shafts. And ghosts.

Using both hands, Rusty picks up the chain. The padlock is already open and falls to the ground as the gate swings open.

"It's as though someone wants us to come in," says Rusty.

Maybe I was right and Sadie and Dexter were herding us, but I don't voice this to Rusty. He looks nervous enough as it is.

With a dry mouth, I step through the open gate.

To say I'm scared is an understatement. I've got cold sweats and I'm sure I can smell BO – although I'm hoping it's Rusty and not me.

The driveway that must lead to the house winds to the left and right, spiny bushes and wind-blown trees closing in around us. They reach out with their leafless, skeleton branches to block the view back to the gate and Greyscar town.

It's eerily quiet.

"What are you thinking?" I ask Rusty, keen to break the silence.

"I'm thinking about Sadie and Dexter and Miss Chen. They're kind of like empty shells just waiting around until the Cinderman takes control of them."

"Exactly!" I say, glad I'm not the only one paying attention. "It's like he's only got enough power to fully control a few of them at the same time. Sadie and Dexter were super-fast, but Miss Chen was pretty much asleep. Until he needs them, everyone is zombified—"

"I think you mean 'ghombified'," interrupts Rusty.

"Ghombified?" I frown.

"Ghost-controlled zombies. Ghombies. I made it up just now."

It's a good name for them.

"Do you think they eat brains?" I ask.

"If they do, you're safe," he replies.

Same old Rusty. He can't resist a joke at my expense.

"Sorry," he mumbles at my back.

Rusty has never apologized to me voluntarily. It usually takes Mum or Dad threatening to confiscate his entire Battle

Beast collection to get a hint of a sorry out of him.

"Did you just—"

"Apologize? Yes. I think so…"

This is a big moment. I could mess this up in an instant by snapping back with something snarky, but I don't. We're going looking for letters revealing the name of a ghost in a haunted house. We're probably about to die horribly. So, instead, I take a deep breath.

"Appreciated."

Rusty grins and we continue together. It actually feels pretty good to be getting along.

The drive narrows and bends and then suddenly we emerge in a small valley, the kind Grandpa would call a dell. It's like something from a fairy tale – a really spine-chilling one – because in the dell is a house and it's the scariest house I've ever seen.

If I had to pick two words to describe it, I'd pick "diseased" and "murderous". The stone is covered in black mould, the front door is rotten and hanging off its hinges and the gaping holes that once held windows remind me of unstitched wounds.

It's huge – three storeys high – but because it's set in this dip in the land it remains hidden like a horrible secret.

"Looks cosy," says Rusty. "Shall we?"

Together, we walk through the doorway. The house is somehow even bigger inside than outside. Ahead, a staircase stretches upwards like the trunk of a huge tree. A landing circles it, rooms branching off it into the gloom.

The hallway where Rusty and I are standing is just as dark and uninviting. Under my feet is a sea of broken black and white tiles, as though a giant has picked up the floor and shaken it out like a rug.

Rusty grabs his head torch, but I stop him turning it on.

"Your eyes will get used to the dark. Save it for emergencies." I know this from multiple animal stake-outs. What I don't add is that it's easier to be aware of what's lurking in the shadows if you aren't focused on the light.

We both put the torches on our heads, so we have them ready for when we need them and take out our cans of lavender air freshener. I really hope it works, but I can't quite believe that stinky spray will be enough.

Fingers on triggers, we crunch our way across the entrance hall, the crackle of tiles beneath my feet setting my teeth on edge.

"This place is huge!" whispers Rusty.

"And creepy," I add. "Let's hope we find the desk with the letters in quickly."

We move through the house together, checking each

room and then meeting in murky hallways to exchange notes. Not that there's much to say. Most of the rooms are bare, just ashy floorboards, bits of broken furniture and unlit fireplaces. Nothing's breathing except maybe some bugs on an eyeless stuffed fox. It's propping open the library door. Even though it's dead, I feel a bit sorry for it being stuck in a place this derelict and forgotten.

I'd imagined the library having row upon row of books stacked all the way to the ceiling, but barely a single book has survived. Ripped and scattered pages cover every available surface. I pick up a torn front cover only to find a bookplate stuck on the reverse showing a black mountain of coal with two hands reaching out of it. One holds what looks like a pickaxe. The other grasps a cross.

Rusty stares at the bookplate. "Lovely family crest."

It's far from lovely, but it is revealing. My pulse quickens.

"The kind of crest a family that owned a mine might have," I say.

Beneath the crest are the words *Ex libris Ashford*.

On the opposite wall hangs an obscenely huge oil painting, twice my height. It shows a hard-faced man in a grey three-piece suit. He's staring straight ahead, shoulders back, chin raised, his right hand resting on a silver skull-topped cane while his left hand grips a teenage boy's shoulder.

The boy is blond and also dressed all in grey. His face is pale, his eyes wide. He looks terrified.

"Friendly looking pair, aren't they?" Rusty whispers in my ear. "Do you think they're the" – he mouths the word – "Ashfords?"

"I'd bet my binoculars on it," I say.

But my eyes are drawn to another smaller painting propped up on the floor, facing the wall. I cross the dusty floorboards and turn it over.

There are four people in this portrait. There's the hard-faced man and the scared-looking teenage boy from before, but this time a woman sits in front of the man on a dark green velvet chair. She's dressed in black, her folded hands so thin you can almost see the bone beneath, but it's the girl next to her that takes my breath away. It's the blond girl from the painting in Miss Chen's house. She's in the same white dress – and those eyes, I'd recognize those bright blue eyes and intense stare anywhere, gazing out at me like they're trying to tell me something.

"Are you okay?" says Rusty. "You look like you've just seen a ghost."

"Ha, ha," I say, turning away. "Yeah, I'm fine."

I'm not. It feels like this painting has been ripped from the wall and tossed aside in anger. The frame is broken, the cloth back ripped, the hanging string frayed. It leaves a horrible taste in my mouth.

I stride back out into the corridor. So far, the house has been as silent as a tomb, which surprises me. Despite it being murky and derelict, and despite the horrible family paintings and the stories, there doesn't seem to be anything ghostly here at all.

Soon we've covered the ground floor and are back in the entrance hall looking up at the sweeping staircase.

"Let's get this over with," says Rusty, heading up the stairs. "This place is seriously sketchy."

I nod and follow him.

It's not until we're halfway up that I hear something. I pause, the wood beneath me groaning in protest, and beneath that is the sound of ticking.

"Do you hear that?"

Rusty nods, his fingers turning white as he tightens his grip on the air freshener.

"The first sign of trouble and we're out," he says.

"Agreed," I say.

The higher we climb, the louder the ticking is, and a creeping sense of unease settles on my shoulders.

There are eight doorways running around the balcony at the top of the stairs. I peek through each one, finding nothing until the last doorway, which leads to a long curving corridor. The ticking is coming from the door at the end; the only door which is shut.

I grasp the brass handle – it's cold to the touch, as though someone has been holding an ice cube against it – and push open the door.

The room is pitch black, the ticking echoing off the walls, rhythmical as a heartbeat.

"I don't like it," whispers Rusty.

Neither do I, but I can't avoid the only room with something in it. We're here for the letters and I'm going to make sure we get them. I didn't give up when everyone said I'd never see a pine marten. It took two years, but I did. I lie to myself that this is the same thing. Only with the threat of ghombification or death hanging over me...

I flick the switch on my head torch. A ray of light shoots across the room. It makes me feel better for precisely two seconds, until I notice what is different about this room.

Everywhere else, the windows are just holes, open to the elements. Here they're boarded up. Is it to keep people out, or to keep something in?

Heart pumping double-time, I pan the torch slowly left and right, taking in blood-red plaster and peeling green wallpaper. There's a desk and a chair at the far end of the room. In the centre, a rug, sunken in the middle as though the floorboards are in the process of eating it.

"Stay here and keep guard," I say, sounding braver than I feel.

Rusty, for once, seems keen to do as he's told. He nods, eyes wide, finger on his air freshener trigger.

Skirting the sunken rug and following the ticking, I hurry across the room to the desk. I don't want to be in this room a moment longer than necessary.

The desk has a fold-out top, hiding ten little drawers at the back with five alcoves above them. I search them all, coming up empty handed, before I remember that Mum bought a desk like this in a car boot sale. She immediately painted it bright yellow, but I wonder if everything else might be the same...

I put down the lavender spray and reach beneath the desk top, feeling for a lever.

Bingo. A hidden drawer slides out. I can't help giving a smile of relief. Even though there aren't any letters in sight, I've found something.

Inside the drawer, on a bed of green velvet, sits a gold pocket watch and a pink cloth-bound book about the size of my palm. I pick the pocket watch up, the chain clinking prettily in my hand. The clock is ticking, but the face is hidden, covered by a case with an engraving on it.

"What is it?" Rusty calls from the doorway.

"Come and see," I say, beckoning him in.

I lower my head torch to look at the inscription.

Rusty leans over and before I can stop him, he reads the inscription out loud, "Colton Ashford."

The moment the words leave his lips, hissing fills the air and ash begins to pour into the room – streaming through the cracks in the ceiling and the floorboards, like sand filling an hourglass.

Banshee's warning comes back to me: *Speak of the devil and you give him power.*

"Rusty, what have you done?" I shout.

I think we're in the Cinderman's house...and Rusty has just powered him up by speaking his real name out loud.

14

"Indigo...watch out...the ash!" Rusty cries.

Shoving the watch and book in my pockets, fear pumping through my veins, I turn to leave, only to find my way is blocked. The ash is piling up in front of me like the remains of a giant bonfire. But instead of burning down and getting smaller, it's getting bigger and denser, taking shape.

Shoulders as wide as gravestones and legs as thick as church pillars form from the seething mass of darkness. Arms ripple out of it, complete with long clawed hands that look sharp enough to slice air.

Time seems to stand still.

I tremble, making the light from my head torch jump and judder, but I don't move away. I can't tear my eyes from this monster of ash and cinder. I'm literally watching a nightmare come alive.

"Run!" Rusty's voice echoes around the room.

But I'm rooted to the spot, mesmerized by and terrified of the creature responsible for Ashmageddon.

The monster lifts its head, turning coal-black eyes on me. They're a set of dead stars, cold and unfeeling, and they chill me to the bone.

"Finally, I am whole," growls that now horribly familiar, ash-choked voice.

It sounds pleased, as though we've played into his hands.

Every instinct is telling me to run, but I can't seem to tear myself away from Colton Ashford, or the thing he has become.

There's a *shushing* sound and the smell of lavender fills the air. It stings my eyes and makes me cough, but the Cinderman roars as though it burns.

"Get away from her!" yells Rusty, finger pressed hard against the canister trigger, a haze of scented gas blasting from the nozzle.

I blink. He's facing off against a giant ashy ghost with only a can of Smell Fresh for protection. His actions are utterly ridiculous, but my heart swells with pride, coupled with an overriding urge to protect him.

What am I doing standing here? My brother just saved me; I need to save him right back.

I rush forwards, ducking beneath the Cinderman's

reaching arms, and out the other side.

"Move!" I yell.

I grab Rusty's shoulder, accidentally knocking the canister to the floor.

The Cinderman turns to give chase and stumbles, unsteady on his new legs, sending an ash cloud billowing into our faces.

Rusty sneezes, but it'll take more than a bit of ash to stop us. While the Cinderman regains his balance, we dive for the door, careering down the hallway, the watch ticking in my pocket, the book pressing into my side.

As soon as we step onto the staircase the scrape of claws sounds behind us. Rusty and I look at each other. There's no need for words. We're being chased.

We take the stairs two at a time, landing in the hallway at the same time as a large, eyeless, red fox.

It's covered in ash, its movements jerky and unnatural, like the ghombified people's. Several black threads dangle from its eyeless sockets.

My eyes widen. I'm not sure how the Cinderman's done it, but he's animated the dead fox from the library to do his dirty work.

The fox growls, pulling back black lips to reveal sharp yellow teeth.

"Move slowly," I whisper to Rusty, feeling in my rucksack for a bath bomb. "If you run, animals always give chase."

"Even stuffed ones?" he wheezes, backing away, feet crunching on the broken tiles.

We edge towards the door, Rusty holding a handful of sage stuffing and me brandishing the bath bomb. The fox snarls and snaps at us from the bottom step but it stays where it is.

We inch over the threshold and slam the front door. It's so rotten the handle comes off in my hand. I'm doubtful this door will stop even a gentle breeze, let alone a possessed fox.

I'm right. The fox leaps through the door as easily as teeth crunching through a wafer and we're running again. Down the ash-strewn driveway, past the skeleton trees, away from the fox, that decomposing nightmare of a house and the Cinderman.

I toss the door handle behind me followed by the salt bomb. The fox leaps the first missile and dodges the second.

It's surprisingly agile for something that looks like it's been overstuffed. It pulls alongside us, as though it's trying to turn us back towards the house and the mine. Rusty throws a handful of sage in its face. The creature pulls back momentarily, and we race ahead.

"Stop if you want to get eaten!" Rusty shouts as the fox snaps at his heels.

Thankfully, the route back to town is downhill and we're closing in on the gates, because my lungs are about to burst.

We've got one chance. If we get there first, maybe, just maybe, we can shut the fox in and us out before it eats us for lunch.

We sprint through the gates side by side, clanging them shut behind us. The fox skids to a halt, then freezes and falls over, stuffing trailing from its back legs. It's as though the fox was a car the Cinderman was driving. Now it's no longer useful to him, he's got out of the driver's seat and abandoned it.

Safe from rabies, I lean against the gates, breathing hard. It's then that despair hits, squeezing at my ribs, making my breath catch in my throat.

Not only did we not get what we came for – the letters – but we've also powered up the Cinderman. He can form a body out of ash now. It's only a matter of time before he comes for us in person instead of sending one of his mindless minions.

I clench my fists, but I can't direct all my anger at my brother. Rusty was the one who said the Cinderman's name, but I was the one who released him in the first place.

What a team. We're meant to be Spooksmiths, keeping people safe from the ghouls lurking in the crypt's urns, and look what we've done.

"It's not all bad," says Rusty, noticing my stony expression. "We didn't get captured, ghombified or torn apart by a reanimated fox. And we got that book and the watch. Maybe they can tell us something?"

I hurriedly flick through the book first, my heart sinking when I find it only contains dried flowers and drawings. It's the kind of thing I'd usually enjoy looking at, but it's no use to us. I shove it back in my pocket, pull out the watch and flick open the lid.

The watch ticks like a normal watch, but the milky white clock face has no hands and is missing most of its numerals. The numbers only range from two to seven...

Why?

I frown and hold it out to show Rusty.

"Seven o'clock tonight is sunset," he says slowly.

As he says it, the wind picks up, carrying an ash-choked voice towards us.

"*Tick tock. Tick tock. You've stolen my watch, now enjoy the countdown.*"

With a shudder, I shove the watch back in my pocket.

15

We cross a deserted Coal Road, hanging our heads.

"What now?" says Rusty.

"We'll go back to Grandpa. We'll make a new plan." I try to sound upbeat, but it's hard to keep the disappointment out of my voice. We might have escaped the Cinderman, but instead of finding the letters and weakening him, we've made him stronger by saying his name.

Ash starts falling from the sky again and I peer into the gloom. We're coming up to the library on Lantern Lane. Salt patches bloom on the bricks and the windowsills sag with age, so you'd never guess that inside it's all shiny and new. But the two blurry figures darting about inside definitely aren't modern: Bernard and Tanvir.

"What are they up to?" I whisper.

Rusty shrugs. "Let's ask them. It feels like going back to the start if we go home with nothing and I'm sure we can get more information out of them."

I don't need persuading. I follow him through the sliding glass doors.

Usually, the library is as busy as a shopping mall. From reading to voting, yoga classes to baby and toddler music club, you name it, you can do it at Greyscar Library. But today all the screens are blank, and the library is darker and quieter than a morgue. Books lie abandoned on tables and kids' toys and instruments are scattered across the playtime rainbow rug. The most friendly and welcoming place in Greyscar suddenly feels like it's had an eerie midnight make-over.

"Hello?" I call out. "Bernard?"

A *thump* sounds from the ceiling above. A thump like a dropped book...

"Tanvir?" calls Rusty. "Is that you?"

"Let's split up and search for them," I suggest.

Rusty nods and disappears down row six and I take row seven. I'm halfway along it when I hear whispered voices.

"*There's nothing here,*" wails Tanvir.

"*Look harder,*" replies Bernard.

Like the *thump* from before, their voices seem to be coming from above my head, but the library doesn't have a second floor...or does it?

"Rusty," I hiss.

Rusty's head appears through a gap in the bookshelf beside me.

"Bernard and Tanvir—" I say.

"—are above us now," interrupts Rusty. "There must be a hidden floor or some sort of attic."

That's one of the many problems with ghosts: they move quickly and don't let little things like solid walls or floors get in their way.

We both follow our rows to the end and meet at the far wall. There's a door marked *Private* and another door to the toilets. We go through the *Private* door. It leads into a dark corridor. The light switch does nothing, so we both flick our head torches on.

There's a kitchen and a meeting room leading off the corridor, but no stairs to a second floor. Although I'm sure a room exists. I can hear Bernard muttering directly above me.

Rusty scans the ceiling with the beam from his head torch and points. There's a small hatch above with a rope attached. Only neither of us can reach it.

I grab a chair from the meeting room, standing on it to

reach the rope. I pull on it and as the hatch opens, a creaky set of ladder steps unfold. They're rickety and dirty, as if no one has used them in a hundred years.

The voices fall silent.

We scramble up the rungs and into a dingy attic. A single blade of light falls through a gap in the cobweb-covered window at the far end. On all sides, curved wooden beams hug the space like the hull of a boat. In between these beams stand tottering piles of dusty books and documents.

"*You,*" hisses shaven-headed, monocle-twitching Bernard.

"*You made it out of Greyscar House alive,*" says Tanvir. "*Thank goodness, I'd have felt so guilty if—*"

"*Did you find the letters?*" interrupts Bernard, rudely.

"No," says Rusty.

"But we did find—"

Bernard cuts me off with a dismissive snort. "*You failed. We don't have time to hear about any trinkets you've picked up. The only items of consequence are those damnable letters. If you haven't got them, then run along. The grown-ups are at work.*"

My fingers curl into fists. Bernard is one of the worst kind of grown-ups, self-important with a sneering, *I know best* attitude, but I need to keep my cool if I want to discover anything useful.

"What is this place?" asks Rusty.

"*I call it the Doomed Library,*" says Tanvir, his eyes filling with tears.

"*Always so dramatic,*" says Bernard, rolling his eyes. "*It's where all the books and documents that nobody wants end up.*"

"*In my time as Head Librarian,*" says Tanvir, "*if a book had not been taken out for over two years it was supposed to be pulped.*" Tanvir's voice cracks on the last word.

"*Sacrilege!*" growls Bernard. "*Books are precious and must be protected at all costs. It's the only thing we agree on.*"

I'm glad to hear that sour old Bernard cares for something.

"*So we saved all the doomed books here,*" Tanvir explains.

"And you're up in this Doomed Library now because you're looking for something…" says Rusty.

"*There's no mention of the Cinderman in the books downstairs, but we think there might be a reference to his real name up here,*" says Tanvir.

"And what will you do if you find it?" I ask.

Tanvir looks shiftily at his feet.

"*Bernard says we must bury it in a locked box,*" he says. "*It will mean no one can read his name and it will also keep the book safe from harm.*"

"But we need to destroy it!" I say.

"*You should be worrying about the letters!*" snaps Bernard. "*Now be off with you!*"

He moves off to check books further down the room.

Tanvir wipes away a cobweb dangling from his turban.

"I wish I could help more..."

"You can," I whisper. "Help us find the book Bernard's looking for."

Tanvir shakes his head. *"You'll destroy it."*

"What if we promise not to?" says Rusty.

"Rusty!" I hiss. "We can't promise that. Grandpa said to get rid of all references to the Cinderman's real name."

"But what if Grandpa's wrong? Maybe now I've said his name out loud the damage is done and it doesn't matter where his name is written down." Rusty blushes as he admits his mistake, but he makes a good point.

"Go on," I say. I don't know if it's linked to my Spooksmith abilities, but something in my gut is telling me Rusty is on to something.

"I've got a feeling we need to find out more about the Cinderman to discover his weakness. In Battle Beast, knowledge of your enemies is key," he continues. "All the Spooksmith advice we've been given has been passed down. None of it is first-hand."

"It's probably not even fourth- or fifth-hand," I say. "Grandpa said everything he knew had been told to him by his grandmother, who'd been told by some other relative.

It's like that game called Telephone, where you whisper a message to the person next to you and they pass it on and so on. The more people the message goes through, the more distorted it gets. By the time it reaches the last person, it's nothing like the original."

"Exactly!" he says. "No one has ever released a ghost from one of the crypt's urns before, which means we're in new territory anyway. We should do things our way. Make our own rules."

I can't deny that this feels like the right thing to do. "Okay," I say. "I won't destroy the book; we'll use it for info. I really don't care how we defeat the Cinderman, I just care that we do."

"*Ah-ha!*" says Bernard, holding up a heavy-looking black leather book.

"Grab it!" I shout.

We both rush Bernard, who screams and disappears through the roof. Unfortunately for him, the book is a solid object and can't go with him. It falls to the floor with a thud, and I snatch it up.

"*You snakes!*" yells Bernard, charging back into the room in a blast of cold air. "*And you!*" he yells threateningly at Tanvir.

But before Bernard can rush me, he freezes. He reminds me of a deer caught in car headlights.

"What is it?" I ask.

And then I hear it. It's soft, like the end of an echo, but as I listen it gets louder and clearer until I can make out hundreds of voices singing together.

"Don't expect a warning,
The Cinderman is calling,
Ashes, ashes,
Speak his name!"

They've changed the last line. It sounds like they're gloating. My blood goes from cold to frozen in an instant.

Rusty and I run for the attic window and wipe away some of the grime. What I see below makes me feel like I've been punched in the chest.

16

The residents of Greyscar are sweeping through the streets chanting the Cinderman nursery rhyme. Shovels, pickaxes and chisel bars are slung over their shoulders, and they are marching as one towards Greyscar House and the mine.

"That's it. He's taken control of everyone. He's won," says Bernard, disappearing through the wall.

"Bernard, wait!" calls Tanvir, disappearing after him.

Rusty turns pale.

"I think I can see Jai down there." He points with a shaking finger at a figure in the crowd.

"They're too far away to be sure," I say.

I put the book I took from Bernard in my rucksack and then we both hurry down the ladder, back to the glass entrance doors at the front of the library.

"They're all here," says Rusty.

I fight the feeling of rising dread building in the pit of my stomach, while he lists the names of our friends, teachers and neighbours as they pass by.

"There's Jai," says Rusty. "And Sam T. They're going to be well impressed when we save everyone, and I tell them they turned ghombie."

He's trying to keep things light, but I can hear the worry in his voice. Whether anyone makes it out alive or not is all on us.

Rusty continues to list names. "Miss Chen, Mr Cane, Sadie, Dexter..."

Hearing Dexter's name is like removing the wrong brick in a game of Jenga – all my carefully contained emotions come crashing down. I can't bear to stand here a moment longer. Without giving it a second thought, I'm outside, diving into the tide of ghombies.

The crowd is robotic, surging relentlessly forward like an army. Their movements are stiff, bodies unyielding. I know that if I fall, they'll trample straight over me, but I'm not letting my nerves get the better of me. I'm not going to fall. I have to make a difference. If I can just save one person...

"Dexter!" I shout, getting in front of him. "Dexter!"

Unlike last time, he doesn't snap out of it. He doesn't react at all and neither do any of the other marchers. Their white eyes just stare straight ahead, and I have to jump out of the way to avoid being stamped on.

I can hear Rusty shouting my name, but it feels like I'm underwater, my eardrums thudding with the sound of my heart and marching feet. Rusty's hands grab my shoulders and pull me back out of the crowd and inside the library.

"What were you thinking?" he shouts.

"I'm sorry!" I sob. "I couldn't stand there and do nothing. The Cinderman was controlling one or two people at a time before, but now he's controlling everyone at once. Bernard's right. We're out of time. We've lost. We're never getting our friends back."

"We've not lost," says Rusty, shaking my shoulders. "And don't you dare take Bernard's word over mine."

I snort-laugh at his last sentence.

"Okay, I promise to believe you over Bernard." I wipe my eyes and nose on my sleeve.

"And don't you ever dive into a crowd of ghombies again without me," he says. "There's no way I want to be the last man standing. If we're going down, we're going down together."

"Deal," I say, and we share an awkward brother–sister hug, where he somehow manages to elbow me in the head. So I jab him in the ribs.

"OW!" he yelps.

"Yeah, let's not do that again." I grin. "Hugging hurts."

"What do you think the Cinderman is up to, getting everyone to march like that?" says Rusty, rubbing his side.

"I don't know, but I liked your idea about finding out more about him so we can discover his weakness." I shrug off my rucksack and pull out the black, Bible-sized book we took from Bernard.

We both sit down at a desk and I put the book on the table.

Rusty reads the title out loud. "*Northern History and the Stories Between*."

I flick through it until I find a chapter called *The Legend of the Cinderman*, and then I start to read, with Rusty peering over my shoulder.

"'The true origins of the Cinderman myth and the well-known nursery rhyme of the same name continue to be a mystery. A strong case could be made for many dastardly figures in history, but my favourite would be—'"

"Don't say his name!" warns Rusty.

"'CA'," I say, shortening the Cinderman's real name to a set of initials.

"'CA was responsible for many deaths and even his own end is questioned. Some believe he fled the country after the last in a long line of accidents in his mine; others that he fell victim to the dangers of the mine himself.

"'One story goes that after the death of several children in a flooded tunnel, the villagers refused to work for him any more. Bereft of workers, CA decided to work the mine himself. It was to be his downfall. When his body was recovered at the bottom of a shaft, there was a gaping cavity where his heart should sit—'"

"What, so his heart just fell out?" says Rusty.

"Hang on," I say, scanning the page. "It suggests here that it was torn out by ghostly miners and then his body was pushed into the pit. Yuck!"

"Intriguing," says Rusty. Worryingly, he's not looking remotely grossed-out. "Go on."

"There's more about what a horrible person he was and the idea that the dead miners ripped out his heart for revenge, to remove any remaining good and leave him a miserable monster... I mean, wow."

"Give it here," says Rusty.

I push the book towards him. He reads on for a minute in silence, before speaking. "Not only did he run a dangerous, child-killing mine, but he left his mum and sister to die in Ashford Asylum. You drive me up the wall, but even I draw the line at that."

"That's really big of you," I say, making sure to lay the sarcasm on heavy. "So, what happened to the heart?"

Rusty stabs the page with his finger. "I guess it's still in the mine."

My brain is whirring a hundred miles a second.

"All the townsfolk were walking towards the mine with pickaxes and digging equipment. I know it doesn't make any sense because it should have rotted away long ago, but do you think...maybe...the Cinderman is looking for his heart?"

"If it has somehow survived, it would make sense that it's more powerful than his name in keeping him anchored to the living world," says Rusty, a smile slowly spreading across his face.

The pieces of information are clicking together in my mind like a giant jigsaw.

"The heart could be his biggest weakness," I add. "And if we can find it and destroy it before the ghombies get it for him..."

"Then maybe we can save Greyscar!" finishes Rusty.

17

The truly mind-boggling scale of our plan – to go to a derelict mine, filled with ghombies, to find and destroy the Cinderman's missing heart – is sinking in. I have no idea how we'll search miles of dark tunnels and avoid certain death and I don't think Rusty does either. We've both fallen silent by the time we reach home. The only thing we do know is that we need to gather more supplies for our journey underground. Hopefully, Grandpa will have some advice and seeing Phrank will cheer us up. Although, things aren't looking promising...

The black front door to the funeral parlour is hanging open, the same as every house we've passed – but unlike every other house, there's ashy graffiti scrawled across the windows:

I am watching you, Spooksmiths.

Hate radiates off the letters like a bad smell. It doesn't feel like an empty threat and my chest tightens. If the Cinderman has hurt Grandpa...or Phrank... We hurry inside, slamming the door behind us.

We walk through the funeral parlour, passing the display urns and the bookcase, and into the main house. It's cold and lifeless. The only sound is the *tick, tick, tick* of the watch in my pocket counting down to sunset.

"Grandpa?" Rusty calls, his voice high and uneven.

No answer.

Fear trickling through my body, I peer into the sitting room. Mum and Dad are gone. The thought that they were in the ghombie crowd with Dexter makes me want to throw up.

"Phrank?" I whisper as I walk down the corridor, heart thudding in time with my steps.

"Please let them be all right," whispers Rusty.

There's a faint chirrup and rustle of packets from the kitchen.

On the table, amongst the cereal packets and angel cake wrapper, sits Phrank, chest puffed out, orange eyes gleaming.

Despite everything I force a smile.

"If he's all right, maybe Grandpa is too," I say.

Rusty looks doubtful, but he starts opening cupboards, filling his bag with spare batteries and snacks.

I pick up a handful of spilled Wheatie Hoops and hold them out towards Phrank. He pecks them straight from my hand, letting me stroke his neck as he feeds. Maybe he senses I need the connection. Whatever his reasons, stroking him fights off my own rising panic. I don't have time for it; we've got to stop the Cinderman. We can't let him win.

I shrug off my rucksack and take a seat at the kitchen table while Rusty continues to pack supplies. I pull out the pink, cloth-bound book I took from Greyscar House. It's palm-sized and chunky, with pages held together with a worn white ribbon. I take a deep breath and open the book.

The Flora of Greyscar
by Ada Grace Ashford

The Cinderman's mother? Sister? The paper feels thick and expensive even though it's yellowed with age. I flick through the pages, hoping for something, *anything* that might help us in our fight against him. Instead, disappointment seeps deeper into my veins with every turn. It's beautiful, but useless. Every inch of paper is filled with pressed flowers, their names carefully copied out beneath them alongside sketches of leaf details and patterns. And there, on the last page, is a stem of dried honeysuckle, its trumpet-like flowers brittle with age, although, somehow, still holding their scent.

I'm just about to abandon the book when Rusty leans over my shoulder.

"What's that?" he says, prodding the last page.

It's stuck down, but with some effort I unpeel it from the back cover to reveal a slim pocket. It's slightly raised, as though there's something stuffed inside.

Hardly daring to hope, I reach in and pull out a thin collection of folded letters.

"No way!" says Rusty. "Do you think they're the letters Bernard sent us to find?"

Fingers clumsy with anticipation, I flatten them out, and Rusty takes a seat beside me. We both read in our heads to avoid saying anything we shouldn't out loud.

April 21ˢᵗ 1858   *Ashford Asylum*
                                                        Greyscar

My dearest brother,
I hate this place. The people who run it are small minded
and mean. Yesterday, I tried to go down to the rose garden,
only to be told it was forbidden because I had tried to pass
a letter to Mother in the corridor. I only wrote the letter
because the doctors will not let me see her or speak to her.
She looks worse than ever, pale and withdrawn, although

it is no wonder, being trapped here. Sometimes I imagine I see her soul clawing at the windows to get out, but I know I should not say things like that because then you will think I deserve to be here, as Father does...

How is Father? There are rumours his health is failing. The orderlies here talk of how you are taking over the running of the estate and the mine. If this is so, then I have hope that Mother and I will not be here much longer.

Please, Colton, no person could be expected to get well here. It is a prison. My greatest wish is to be home for my fourteenth birthday and to sit beneath the apple tree together the way we used to when I was little.

Your devoted sister,

Ada

"The flower book belongs to the Cinderman's sister!" says Rusty.

She sounds like everything that her monstrous brother isn't – kind and caring and full of life. My heart is beating faster as more pieces of the puzzle fall into place.

"I have a feeling she's the blond girl in the portrait at Greyscar House," I say.

"And maybe the sussy-looking guy in the other portrait is her father and the teenage boy is you-know-who," says Rusty.

I nod.

"There's more."

There are five other letters from Ada, so we read on. Each time she writes, her words are less generous, less warm. The final letter is dated almost a year later, and the tone couldn't be colder if it tried.

February 6th 1859   *Ashford Asylum*

                                                          Greyscar

Dear Colton,

Mother is dead and I am to assume that you have chosen to leave me to the same fate. My letters have gone unanswered even though I warned you the fever is spreading here. I have heard about the dreadful conditions at the mine. I wonder if that is why you wish me gone. God forbid that you should have a weak-minded sister holding you back from your worst excesses and reminding you to be kind. Soon you will be alone with only your wealth and power for company. I will not trouble you again, but I cannot but hope that your conscience prevails. Deep down I know you have a heart. For your sake, please listen to it before it is too late.

Yours,

Ada Grace Ashford

Carefully, because the paper is delicate and my hands are trembling, I fold the letters back up and return them to the pocket.

"What kind of a monster keeps his sister's letters, but refuses to save her life?" I ask.

"A really sick one," says Rusty.

I'm sure there's more to unpick from the letters, but I'm finding it hard to focus. There's a strange rustling noise coming from the chimney, like a bird has fallen behind the panelling and is struggling to get out.

"Grandpa?" calls Rusty.

There's no reply. Where is he, and what's causing that sound?

"I don't like it," I say.

"Me either. It's making me all angsty."

The rustling gets louder and Rusty and I back away as ash starts to creep between the gaps in the boards.

It can't be... Not *him*... Not here... Not in our home...

The panelling buckles and ash explodes into the room, surrounding us in a swirling tornado, carrying with it that ash-choked voice.

"*Spooksmiths must pay for their crimes,*" hisses the Cinderman. The ash pools together to create legs and arms and a body that isn't quite human.

My heart is in my mouth and my skin feels like it's being sandblasted. I hold my hands over my face to protect it, but there's nowhere left to run. The Cinderman has come for us.

"Never again will I be trapped," he hisses.

Both Rusty and I are pinned to the spot, frozen with fear. But not Phrank. Without a moment's hesitation, he launches himself at the Cinderman, squawking and screeching with all the fury of a guard dog.

There's a sharp bark of ghostly laughter – it's a horrible sound, like the crack of breaking bone – and the ash swirls away from me. It blasts Phrank into the open broom cupboard, where he lands against the hoover.

How dare he hurt Phrank! My anger unfreezes me and I run to help him. Phrank squawks as if to say he's okay and pecks at the hoover. He looks at me. Clever bird! It's an audacious plan, but it's worth a shot. Phrank takes flight and I grab the hoover. It's already plugged in, so as the Cinderman rushes me, I dash out into the kitchen, trailing the power cable.

Rusty finally grasps the situation and switches the hoover on as I aim the nozzle.

The Cinderman roars as his head disappears up the hose into the vacuum cleaner. I whoop because I can't believe this is working.

"If we'd done this at the start," yells Rusty, "we wouldn't be having all this trouble now!"

Mum and Dad always make vacuuming look such a chore. Who knew it could be so satisfying?

A muffled roar comes from the hoover bag, but I don't stop. I suck up his arms, legs and every last scrap of ash in the kitchen until I can see the red sides of the hoover bulging and warping like an overblown balloon.

The sides stretch wider and wider and the hoover starts to groan.

I should have known it wouldn't be this easy.

"It's gonna blow!" yells Rusty.

"Take cover!" I shout.

Rusty and I leap for the broom cupboard, followed by a madly flapping Phrank.

With a *creak* followed by a *BANG*, the vacuum cleaner explodes, firing ash in every direction as I slam the cupboard door shut.

18

Rusty and I huddle in the dark of the cupboard with Phrank, listening to the hiss of swirling ash outside.

"Why is the Cinderman here?" whispers Rusty, his voice wavering. "He only needs to wait until sunset and he's won."

Spooksmiths must pay for their crimes. Those were the words he used and as they sink in, I nearly choke on my own saliva.

"He's not here to fight us because he thinks we're a threat," I whisper. "He's here to punish us."

Rusty curls up smaller. "What's he going to do to us?"

I put a hand on his shoulder. I don't know what the Cinderman can do to us, although I doubt it's anything good.

"We're Spooksmiths," I whisper, gathering my

last shreds of bravery. "Somehow, we've got to fight back."

The ash falls silent as if the Cinderman has been listening.

And then I hear Grandpa's voice.

"*Indigo? Rusty?*"

"Grandpa?" says Rusty. He jumps up, putting his hands against the rough wooden slats of the cupboard door. "Is that really you?"

It sounds like him, but where's he been?

"*I'm sorry. I'm so sorry.*" His voice is small and weak. It tugs at my heartstrings.

"Sorry for what, Grandpa?" says Rusty and before I can stop him, he opens the door.

The Cinderman and the ash have gone. There's just Grandpa standing beneath the flickering spotlights, but I hesitate to go to him because things feel wrong. Rusty must sense it too, because even he's holding back.

For a start, Grandpa is standing beside the table with his back to us. His blue suit trousers and pink shirt are all wrinkled and tinged an ashy grey, the edges of his ghostly form quivering.

"Grandpa?" says Rusty.

Grandpa turns around and any hope I had shrivels like a dying flower.

His eyes are white, his mouth pulled into a nasty smile.

When he speaks again, it's not Grandpa's voice. It's the Cinderman's.

"*I can hurt you by hurting the ones you love.*"

Pain tears through my chest. I whimper like a wounded animal, pressing myself up against the kitchen wallpaper until I feel the raised print against my back.

"Why are you doing this?" whispers Rusty.

"*Because I can. I needed you to say my name – why do you think your friends stopped chasing you? Who do you think unlocked the gates to Greyscar House?*"

The Cinderman's gloating tone makes me feel small and stupid and hearing it come from Grandpa's mouth makes it even worse.

"*Now my real name has been spoken by a Spooksmith, I'm too strong to be stopped. When the sun sets it will mark a new beginning. I will be restored as the Lord of Greyscar and my ash haze will ensure this town is never seen by the outside world again. It will be as though it never existed. It and you will be forgotten. Then, Spooksmith powers or not, I will wear you down until you beg me to end your miserable lives.*"

Without a backwards glance, Grandpa drifts away through the closed door and out into the darkening day.

We've lost him. Again.

Rusty slides down the wall onto the floor into a crumpled

heap. He looks like I feel, like a punctured football. All the fight has leaked out of him.

How could we ever have thought we could beat the Cinderman? It's all been pointless. He said it himself, he's too strong.

Exhausted, I lean against the wall and shut my eyes.

Phrank jabs at my school shoes with his beak.

"Go away," I mumble.

Phrank chirrups and pecks at my foot again.

"Stop it."

He doesn't stop. Instead, he aims his beak through the punch-hole detailing on the front of my shoe, hitting the soft skin on the top of my foot.

"Phrank!" This time, I sit up properly. "That hurt!"

He looks at me with his orange, unblinking eyes as if to say *So?* and then, unbelievably, he goes to peck me again.

I move my foot and stand up.

"We've lost, don't you get it?"

Of course, he doesn't get it. He's no sidekick. He's just a tame pheasant with a very peck-happy beak.

I'm about to tell him to bog off, when Phrank cocks his head at the flower book. It's lying on the floor, pushed up against the skirting board, where it must have landed when the Cinderman attacked.

If Phrank was human, I'd say it was a very deliberate sort of look.

I pick up the book. The pale pink cover and white ribbon are stained grey with ash, but it's still intact.

Rusty gives a sniff.

"Why would the Cinderman keep his sister's dried flower book?" he asks.

Was it just a way to hide the letters or is there more to it?

Flicking through the pages, my mind turns over everything I've been through and everything I've learned. When Grandpa died, I felt the loss, but it didn't make me appreciate Mum or Dad or Rusty any more. It somehow just highlighted how different we were. But now they've gone, and all I'm left with is Rusty...the thought of losing him too...

"Maybe the mine wasn't the only thing he loved," I whisper.

"Maybe he didn't realize how much he cared for his sister until she was gone," Rusty adds.

There's an awkward silence, like when Rusty invited Jai over and he admitted he didn't like gravy or Yorkshire puddings. Thankfully, Rusty breaks it by blowing his nose loudly on his sleeve.

"Even if he did care about his sister, what use is it?" He sighs.

Rusty might not be able to see the full picture yet, but I think I can.

"If his heart *has* survived all this time in the mine, maybe Ada is the reason why. Maybe whatever love he had for her has somehow kept it from rotting away? The library book said the ghostly miners ripped the heart out to remove any remaining good. I think she's the good. If his weakness in life was Ada, then surely he has the same weakness in death..."

"So, you're saying underneath all that evil and ashy Lord of Greyscar stuff, he's just a big-hearted softie?"

I grin. "Yeah, that's what I'm counting on."

Phrank chirrups. It sounds a bit like he's saying, *Finally,* and he waddles to the front door.

"Just give me a minute," I say, pulling off my red school jumper. "If I'm about to die looking for a heart in a mine, I really don't want to do it in my school uniform."

I run back upstairs and rifle through the clothes under my bed, looking for my navy cargo trousers and army-green shirt. Instead, I find the yellow boiler suit Mum left for me. I remember the note and the expectation that I would love it. And the way I grimaced and shoved it under the bed...

What the hell.

This is for you, Mum.

I take off my uniform and pull the boiler suit on, tucking

the flower book and the pocket watch into one of the pockets. Then I put on my black Dr. Marten boots.

Next, I raid the bathroom, grabbing the last of the salt bombs and a half-finished can of lavender air freshener. No one other than Rusty would have thought to use Mum's "smellies" as a ghostbusting weapon. I'm going to try harder to appreciate him.

Rusty and Phrank are waiting at the bottom of the stairs. Rusty hands me my rucksack and I shove the bombs and spray into it.

"Girly gravedigger," says Rusty, taking in my new boiler-suited look. "Very fitting."

"Thank you," I say, and I mean it. I take out the pocket watch and check the time.

"Three hours until sunset."

"Three hours to find the Cinderman's heart," Rusty says. "I think we might need an army. What do you say to asking the Little Hope Graveyard ghosts for help?"

I nod my agreement.

"It's going to be the Cinderman's funeral," I say.

Rusty opens the door, and the darkening, ashy afternoon pours into the hallway.

"Or ours," he adds.

19

The conversation with the ghosts of Little Hope Graveyard isn't going quite as I'd imagined it would. Despite my previous not entirely positive experiences with them, I'd somehow convinced myself they would be way more helpful this time around.

"*No,*" snaps Bernard. "*It is too late. We're doomed!*"

"Did you listen to anything my sister just said?" yells Rusty. "We're not doomed yet, but we blummin' well will be if you don't get off your ghostly bottoms and help us find his missing heart!"

We've built up quite the audience. The temperature keeps dropping as more and more ghosts flood into the crypt to listen.

"*What do they mean when they tell Chuckles they've lost everyone? Where are their parents?*"

"The Cinderman has taken control of them," explains Banshee.

"And the friendly ghost who used to wave at Chuckles from the kitchen window?"

"Their grandfather has been taken too," says Banshee.

Chuckles sniffs as though he might be about to cry. He climbs on top of his sarcophagus, motioning to the crowd to quieten down.

"Chuckles will help!" He gives Rusty a gappy-toothed grin.

I feel totally awful for thinking of Chuckles as a creep. He's the only one who's stepped up. Rusty obviously feels the same, because he opens his arms.

"Come on then," says Rusty.

Chuckles doesn't need to be told twice. He throws himself into Rusty's arms, taking a seat on my brother's hip before sticking his thumb in his mouth.

There's a load of ghostly whispering followed by a sharp blast of cold air as Banshee steps in front of me. She hovers there, long dark hair over her face, dirty white gown shimmering with seaweed and slime. She looks like a demon of death and decay.

"We have watched you try and fail and try and fail..."

Wow, this is some pep talk.

"We might have messed up a few times," I say.

"We all agree that it is foolhardy to try and stop the Cinderman, but we applaud your spirit—"

"Not all of us do," mutters Bernard, who is obviously still holding a grudge about me taking that book from him in the library.

Banshee silences him with a dead-eyed stare.

"You cannot make things worse – and you have obviously convinced Chuckles. Tell us what you need."

It's not the uplifting show of support I was after, but a girl's got to take what a girl can get.

I try not to cower in front of Banshee. She looks as though she's fresh from a crime scene. I push my shoulders back and force the words out.

"What we need is for you to create a distraction to lure the ghombies out of the mine—"

"Ghombies?" asks Banshee.

"Ghost-controlled zombies," explains Rusty. "Ghombies."

Banshee frowns like she doesn't get it.

"Never mind," I say. "As I was saying before, we need you to create a distraction so that Rusty and I can find the Cinderman's missing heart—"

"The devil took it," says a voice at the back of the room.

"That evil organ was so rotten it exploded," says another.

"I do not care how it happened. I just hope it caused him

agonizing pain," hisses Banshee.

It's decidedly tricky to get a big group to focus. I don't know how teachers do it.

I look at Rusty and he takes over.

"Indigo and I believe that the heart was ripped out by ghostly miners and is still in the mine. We also think that it is his weakness."

The ghosts grumble between themselves.

"Think about it," I say. "The Cinderman becomes all powerful at sunset so why isn't he just sitting around doing nothing? He must know there's a way to stop him. That's why he keeps trying to break me and Rusty by taking the people we care about. That's why he has all the ghombies going to the mine with pickaxes and shovels."

Silence.

I can see I'm going to have to spell it out.

"Don't you get it? He's using the ghombies to search for his missing heart."

"*So, if we find his heart before he does...*" says Banshee.

"Maybe we can stop him for ever," says Rusty.

"*We will get you both to the mine and lure out the people under his control,*" says Banshee. "*But finding the heart is up to you.*"

Is it me, or is Banshee sounding just a tiny bit positive?

Finally, it seems like things are looking up and we might just have that army Rusty spoke of: a ghost army. As impossible as it seemed an hour ago, it's all actually coming together.

Tanvir clears his throat. *"I don't mean to be difficult, but how will you find the heart?"*

This is the part of the plan that we haven't figured out yet, but I don't want to show our newly assembled army that their leaders are literally in the dark.

"We're Spooksmiths," I say, hopefully styling it out and sounding more confident than I feel.

"Yeah, we've got it covered," says Rusty, deliberately not meeting my eyes.

"And what about after you find the heart?" challenges Bernard, crossing his arms. *"What will you do with it?"*

"Um—" I begin.

"Indigo and Rusty will tear that godforsaken organ to shreds!" roars Banshee. *"But if they cannot bring themselves to do it, then they will bring it to me, and I will devour it!"*

The assembled ghosts fall quiet. Banshee has enough stone-cold rage to literally silence the dead and Rusty and I exchange a look that says, *Let's not argue with her.*

"My daughter died when that tunnel flooded," Banshee explains, swaying in the air as she tells her story. *"She was supposed to be working above ground. He sent her down there to*

her death. I could not even find her body. Finally, I will have my revenge!"

Banshee is officially terrifying even when she's on your side.

"I'm sorry for your loss," I say. "I really am. But if we want to save our parents and everyone in Greyscar, we really need to get to that mine."

"I understand," says Banshee and suddenly Rusty and I are surrounded by a cold damp mist and I feel my feet leaving the floor.

"Now we fly!" giggles Chuckles, still clinging to Rusty.

"Try not to think too much about it," says Banshee.

"Try not to think too much about it?" screeches Rusty, screwing up his eyes so he doesn't have to look down at the fast-disappearing ground. "We've got a hauntorage!"

Rusty might not have a head for heights but I'm loving it. The ghosts lift us up and out of the crypt, through the sinkhole, until we're hovering above the graveyard.

We're flying. Literally flying like a bird. A large ungainly bird, but we're airborne.

Phrank flaps alongside me – he refused to come into the crypt because he'd found something to gobble in all the ash – and I grin. I've often wondered how it would feel to stretch out my arms and fly. If it wasn't for the monster, the mine and the missing heart lying in wait for me – and the starless, ash-filled night smelling of a thousand bonfires – I could get used to this.

20

My stomach somersaults as the ghosts lift Rusty and me higher, up and over Bat Lane towards the wasteland, the mine and Greyscar House. Rusty keeps his eyes squeezed tightly shut. He's shivering. Maybe it's from the cold or the thought of what's waiting for us.

"Are you okay?" I ask.

"Just tell me when it's over," he says.

I can't resist a glance back towards home. I can just make out Serenity Funerals on the hill through the gloom, but home doesn't look like home any more. The whole of Greyscar looks like an unloved toy town from up here; the bright homes, shops and offices are now dark, lifeless boxes. There's no wildlife to liven it up either, no squirrels or nesting birds or seals cruising our coastline. Every single animal has disappeared. The Cinderman has taken everything, not only from me and Rusty, but from everyone in Greyscar. And it's up to us to find a way to take it all back.

Responsibility weighing heavy on my mind, I grit my teeth and turn back to face my future.

As we clear the gates and railings, I spot Greyscar House and beyond that a collection of collapsed buildings and shacks surrounding the mine entrance. It looks intimidating, even from up here. As we get closer, I can see abandoned tools and bits of machinery poking out of the ground like rusty knives.

Every part of my body is screaming *Don't go down there* and that's before the mouth of the mine comes into view. It's a gaping hole of never-ending night.

"*Weeee!*" giggles Chuckles as we come in to land, not letting the seriousness of the situation get in the way of a little fun.

The task ahead feels crushingly enormous. Like I've just been told to climb Everest pursued by wolves while carrying my brother on my back.

Banshee and her ghostly crew set us down at the entrance to the mine and Rusty slowly opens his eyes.

"At least there's no sign of any ghombies," says Rusty.

"Not sure that's a good thing," I say. "It must mean they're all below ground. Where we're going..."

"Great," says Rusty.

Banshee places an ice-cold hand on his shoulder.

"Your chances of success are slight, but we will do our best to ensure you can search for the heart without being followed."

"You're getting sooo good at these encouraging talks," says Rusty.

I hide a giggle.

"I am trying to be more positive," says Banshee.

She motions to the other ghosts. There must be over a hundred of them – some billowing phantoms, others skinny wraiths, none of whom I recognize other than Chuckles, Bernard and Tanvir. On her signal, they all race into the mine, hooting and hollering, all except Chuckles, who remains with Rusty and Banshee.

Within moments, I can hear ghombie shouts mixed with ghostly screams.

"Stand back, but be ready," says Banshee. *"Large groups of people under ghost control are blunt instruments incapable of original thought – the Cinderman does not have enough power to allow each to act individually all at once. As soon as the ghosts chase the people outside the mine, it's your chance to sneak in."*

"How will you keep them busy and stop them getting back into the mine?" asks Rusty.

"*I...I...do not know*," says Banshee, as though the thought hadn't occurred to her.

"That settles it," says Rusty. "I think I should stay and help strategize. I'm the only one with battle experience."

"*You have 'battle experience'?*" says Banshee, looking doubtful.

"I've commanded hundreds of armies," says Rusty, chest puffed out.

"Battle Beast armies," I whisper.

"Trust me. I've got this," says Rusty. He turns to Banshee. "Can you tell all your ghosts to steal the ghombies' equipment? Keep them busy?"

"*Of course*," says Banshee.

"You are now my second-in-command," he says, before giving another load of orders for Banshee to deliver.

I hesitate to leave him, but if anyone is going to be okay, it will be Rusty. He sounds capable, like a proper General, and I feel something that might be pride.

"Make sure you come back," says Rusty. "Or I'll turn your bedroom into my war room."

"That is not happening!"

"I know," he says. "I just wanted to provide an extra bit of motivation. Good luck in there."

"Good luck out here."

A knot tightens in my stomach. I hurry away before I get all soppy and embarrass myself, ducking down behind one of the collapsed buildings to wait for the ghombies to emerge.

Tick, tick, tick, goes the watch in my pocket, reminding me that there's a deadline.

I take it out and flip the lid. It's five o'clock. Two hours until sunset. Two hours to find the heart.

The first groups of ghombies come shuffling out of the mine, furiously swatting at the ghosts, who grab their tools and nimbly dance out of their way. It's like watching greenfly trying to fight off a wasp attack.

When I think most of the townsfolk have been lured out, Rusty gives me a nod.

It's all on me now.

Fighting my quivering nerves, I duck beneath the *KEEP OUT* sign at the entrance and slip into the mine. The darkness is all encompassing, making me feel very small and alone. I hold out for as long as I can and then, when I can't see even a glimmer from the entrance, I put on my head torch.

My heart is hammering way too loudly, and my senses are on high alert. The slightest noise will make me hit the roof. Literally. One jump and I'll bump the ceiling. The tunnel is so low my hair is brushing against the rock above.

A clawing sound echoes against the rock behind me, and I

break into a crouched scramble without looking back.

Either the ghombies have somehow already found me, or some other creature is on to me. What if I'm wrong and all the animals haven't left?

What if it's ghombie rats?

The clawing turns to swooshing.

Or ghombie bats?

Much as I love animals, even I draw the line at ghombie versions.

Without breaking stride, I reach into one of the boiler suit's many pockets and pull out my trusty can of air freshener.

The light from my head torch shows solid rock ahead and a passageway to my right. I grit my teeth and sprint for the turning, the swooshing getting louder with every step.

I swing into the passageway, spin around and take aim. Before I can fire, a flurry of feathers hits me in the chest.

I scream and fall backwards, hitting the rocky ground with a thump.

"Phrank!"

In all the commotion, I hadn't realized he'd followed me.

Phrank chirrups and stares down at me with his beady orange eyes. He seems to be saying, *What are you doing down there?*

I get up, rubbing my bruised bum cheeks. There's no point

being mad. Greyscar Mine is not the kind of place to be alone. It feels both too big – who knows how far the tunnels stretch? – and too small – is it me or is the roof getting lower? Did I also mention the cold and the dark and the mouldy damp smell similar to the crypt under my house?

My head torch picks out three tunnels ahead: identical black holes of nothing.

I turn to Phrank. "Any thoughts?"

Phrank ruffles his feathers and cocks his head, listening.

There's only the sound of my breathing, the quiet ticking of the pocket watch and the *drip, drip, drip* of water. I strain my ears but there's nothing more and my head starts to pound. What can Phrank sense that I can't? I close my eyes and concentrate on slowing my breathing. And then I hear it, a whisper softer than the rustling of a field mouse. It's impossible to make out what it's saying, but it's coming from the left-hand tunnel.

"You, Sir Phrank, are a marvel! Come on!"

The tunnel slopes down until we hit water, ankle deep. Phrank takes off, gliding gracefully above it, leaving me to splash on through like a clumsy pit pony. It's so cold it numbs my toes. I'm grateful when, twenty stomps later, the ground rises, leaving the water behind. I run hard to warm up, following the whisper.

There's another turning and another tunnel.

And another.

And another.

Trying not to think about the weight of rock pressing down above me, I run on, even though my side is cramping with a stitch. Phrank doesn't seem to be enjoying the mine much either. When he lands, his little legs are moving so fast they blur, like he can't wait to get this over with.

The roof drops down again and soon I'm almost doubled over, knees bent in a never-ending squat that makes my thighs burn and my knees ache. I still can't make out what the whisper is saying, but I swear it's getting closer.

Phrank disappears around the next corner and screeches.

My pulse quickens. I round the turning at full speed only for the light from my head torch to bounce back at me. Ahead is a wall of coal. I skid to a halt just before I run into it.

Phrank chirrups from his perch on a rocky shelf. I lift my foot to take a step towards him and he loses the plot, screeching and flying at my head and pulling my hair.

"What's your problem?" I stumble backwards, swatting at him, accidentally knocking my head torch.

The strap slips off my head and the head torch falls.

And it keeps falling.

My skin turns clammy as I stare into the jagged, man-sized hole at my feet, the torch blinking up at me like a distant star. The drop is at least the height of four Rustys standing one on top of the other.

The darkness presses in on me and I mumble a curse. Although it could have been worse. If Phrank hadn't warned me... If I'd fallen instead of the torch... I shiver.

A small voice echoes up from the depths of the pit, so pure it gives me goosebumps. It's weak, but constant, like an audio file stuck on repeat. And it's saying the same word over and over again:

"*Ada.*"

Not a word, but a name. For the first time in a long time, my fear is tinged with excitement.

I think I've found the Cinderman's heart.

21

"**D**on't suppose you fancy flying down there and getting the heart for me?"

Phrank eyes the hole and gives a single, short chirrup from the safety of his perch.

"I'll take that as a no."

The drop looks the height of the stairs at home – without the stairs – but it's not like I have the luxury of endless time to decide whether climbing into a pit within a tunnel deep underground is a good idea. The *tick, tick, tick* of the pocket watch reminds me of that.

I sit down and then slide onto my stomach, shuffling backwards until my legs dangle into the void. With my left leg, I feel for the side, relieved to discover the rock is roughly cut with plenty of places to find a foot- or handhold. I'm a decent climber, so I work my way down quickly, following that repeated whispered word:

"*Ada.*"

The first thing I do when I reach the bottom is to grab the torch from where it fell. Grateful it didn't break, I put it back on my head, spinning around to follow the sound of the voice and to take in my new surroundings.

There's not a lot to take in.

If I stretched out on the floor, I could touch both walls. It's like being at the bottom of a well. If wells could talk...

"*Ada.*"

That voice again, sweet and innocent, beckoning me closer. It's coming from a hole in the rock above my head.

Phrank squawks, no doubt telling me to get on with it, but I hesitate. I've never held a human heart before. Never mind a whispering, supernatural one.

Standing on tiptoes, I exhale and reach inside the crevice, the voice becoming more urgent. My fingers crawl forward until I'm up to my elbow in cold black rock. My breathing is shallow.

Tentatively, I reach further inside the crevice until I feel a small, dry, leathery something.

"*Ada, Ada, Ada,*" goes the whisper, urging me on.

My breath catches in my throat. It feels like I've

found a mummified mouse.

I pull my arm out and unfurl my fingers, peering at the blackened lump in my hand.

The torchlight plays off the nooks and crannies, dips and rises of this once life-giving organ. I've seen human hearts in textbooks, so I know that's what it is even though it's shrivelled to the size and weight of a small pine cone. I can't believe the stories were true. I can't believe I was the one to find it, against all the odds.

"*Ada,*" the heart whispers, and an overwhelming sense of sorrow flows from it into me, years of heartache and repression and fear; fear of what Colton Ashford the man did and of the Cinderman he has become. It's a reminder that even monsters have hearts. And that the Cinderman was human. Once.

I go to put it in my pocket and feel the flower book nestled there. The heady, vanilla scent of honeysuckle fills the air and a vision of the blond girl from the portrait with the piercing blue eyes flares in my brain.

I think it, and the heart confirms it: "*Ada.*" The Cinderman's heart is crying out for his sister. The one good influence in his life. The person that he abandoned but couldn't quite forget. That's why he kept her letters and the flower book with the honeysuckle...

The final piece of the mystery falls into place. Why didn't I think of it before?

The honeysuckle-covered grave in the churchyard... Could it be Ada's final resting place?

My own heart is beating fast now. I think Rusty might be right. Destroying things feels wrong. Maybe destroying the Cinderman's heart is not the answer. Maybe I need him to remember what it feels like to care, to remind him that he wasn't always this way. I need him to remember Ada. And the only way I can think to do that is to take the heart to her grave and hope that remembering what it feels like to love someone will be enough for him to stop Ashmageddon.

"I've got it!" I shout up to Phrank, slipping the heart into my pocket.

Without waiting for an answering chirrup, I climb towards the thick darkness above. The rock feels cold against my skin and my breath clouds in the torchlight, but I'm excited. I've done the hard part; I've found the heart. All I have to do is to make sure the ghombies and the Cinderman don't find me so I can get the heart to Ada's grave before sunset.

It's not until I reach the tunnel above that I notice how quiet it is. The heart has stopped saying Ada's name. Phrank is silent. Even the watch seems to be ticking more quietly.

The torchlight flickers and I freeze, half in, half out of the hole, taking in the ghostly drop in temperature and the unmistakable scent of ash.

My neck is stiff and unwilling, as though it knows I won't enjoy what I'm about to see. I force my head and the flickering torchlight upwards.

Phrank has gone from his perch and is nowhere to be seen. A churning wall of ash borders the edges of the hole. It fills every inch of the tunnel – a dense, hateful darkness that sucks in the light and reflects nothing back.

"*Give me what is mine.*" The Cinderman's voice is all around me, echoing out of the swirling ash.

Butterflies of terror dance around my insides like when I revised for the wrong maths test at school. Times one thousand.

"*Ada,*" whispers the heart fearfully.

I put my hand on it, instinctively protective, but the Cinderman doesn't react to the heart's whispering. I don't think he can hear it.

"Why do you want it?"

"*I cannot stand to know it exists.*"

I can hear disgust in his voice, and another emotion I can't quite place. What I do know is that if he wants to destroy it, then I'm right in wanting to protect it. My Spooksmith instincts are telling me to get the heart to Ada's grave.

Then the ash starts to swirl, creating a buzzing like swarms of flies around a dead animal. Inside the buzzing are eight words:

"Crush it.

Crumble it.

Turn it to dust."

Putting my hands over my ears, I crumple on to the cold, hard ground, wincing as his words burrow into my head like maggots into a corpse. And then I realize what the other emotion is in his voice.

Fear.

His words are eating away at me, but I manage to take the heart out of my pocket. The buzzing stops. The quiet is like the best song I've ever heard.

The heart sits in my hand, a silent and shrivelled black lump of muscle. The ash draws nearer and then flinches away. It's hard to read reactions in something with no eyes. Or mouth. But if I had to guess, I'd say the Cinderman was scared, afraid to touch his heart himself.

"Ada," pleads the heart, its voice so small it's barely even a whisper.

"Destroy it," growls the ash.

It would be easy. The heart is so light and fragile – like a baby bird – one squeeze could kill it... But I am nothing like him. And the fact that he fears it confirms everything I need to know: his heart is his weakness.

"No," I whisper.

The buzzing returns and fighting against it, I put the heart back in my pocket.

"It's never too late to turn things around," I whisper, remembering the last piece of advice Grandpa gave me.

The Cinderman roars and the roar creates an echo that makes the surrounding rock rumble. When the roaring stops, the rumbling doesn't. It gets louder and louder, juddering stones loose from the ceiling. With a shudder, the wall behind me starts to crumble. My own heart pounding, I watch the ash pull back and I realize with a stomach-churning jolt that it's too late for me. The Cinderman has decided to destroy me along with his heart. All I can think about is that I'll never get to argue with Rusty or hug Mum and Dad again.

I scream in fear and pain and frustration as the tunnel caves in, burying me under tons of dirt and stone and rock.

My head torch shatters and darkness floods my brain.

22

I gasp myself awake. It's dark, everything hurts, and my ears are ringing. Muffled voices are telling me to crawl forward, but I feel too trapped and panicky to move. Solid rock is millimetres from my nose and mouth, bouncing every breath back at me, but looking on the bright side, I haven't been crushed. The rocks must have fallen at an angle, leaving a tiny pocket of space.

Screaming feels like the most natural thing to do – if I wasn't too scared to make a sound.

The voices are getting more and more urgent. Eventually, my left ear stops ringing long enough for me to hear someone call my name. I try to call back to them, but my mouth is clogged with dust and dirt and all I manage is a cough.

I inch forwards towards the voice. Every move is painful. Glass-sharp gravel and stones dig into my hands, knees and stomach, while the rock above scrapes and scratches my back. It feels like I'm trying to squeeze through the holes in a cheese grater.

"Keep going."

"*Hurry.*"

Muffled voices call to me as I scrape my body forwards towards a small pinprick of light. It gets bigger the further I crawl and then there's light and space around me, hands on my shoulders and Rusty's voice telling me it's going to be okay.

"You found me," I sob.

"All we had to do was follow Phrank's chirping," says Rusty.

Phrank chirrups and I reach out and stroke his velvety feathers. I thought I'd lost him too.

"I can't believe you came after me," I say.

"Banshee seemed to have everything under control—"

I throw my arms around Rusty, squeezing him so tight.

"Thank you," I say.

"You'd haunt me if you died," he says. "I don't think I could stand that. You're bad enough when you're solid, but the thought of you drifting through walls, all creepy and cold... Yuck."

I laugh and punch him on the arm. I'm just starting to feel

better when a freezing mist wraps around my legs. My heart stutters.

"The Cinderman—" I start to say, but when I look up it's not him. Two ghostly children step into the torchlight.

"Meet Ivy and Freddie," says Rusty. "They led me to you."

Ivy looks about ten years old, her see-through skin stained with coal dust. "*Is it true?*" she asks. "*You have the Cinderman's heart?*"

The heart.

My blood pumps faster as I reach into my pocket, hoping and praying the heart is still in one piece. It is, and not only that, but somehow the dried honeysuckle from the flower book has entwined a slender stem around the dry leathery surface of the heart. It's like it's trying to protect it.

"Is that it?" asks Rusty, peering into my cupped hand.

"*Ada,*" answers the heart, the air filling with that sweet vanilla scent.

"Is it me or did it just speak?" Rusty looks both awestruck and horrified.

"It's calling for the one person the Cinderman felt any love for," I explain. "It's calling for his sister and we are going to be the ones to reunite them."

"Of course we are," says Rusty, shaking his head in disbelief as I return the heart to my pocket. "Nothing can surprise me any more. But what about Banshee? We promised to destroy the heart. In fact, I think she was looking forward to eating it."

"Trust me," I say, taking out the pocket watch to check the time. "We've got just over an hour to get it to Ada's grave in Little Hope Graveyard. And if that fails, I'll feed the heart to Banshee myself."

"Transporting body parts," says Rusty. "Couldn't think of anything I'd rather be doing. I'm in."

"*No one knows these tunnels like us,*" says Freddie, a worryingly thin ghost boy with a face that looks older than he probably is. "*We'll take you to the entrance of the mine.*"

The ghosts go ahead, and Rusty and I follow. Phrank sits on my shoulder like a storybook parrot, chuntering discontentedly along with the endless *tick, tick, tick* of the pocket watch. It's a constant reminder that time is not on our side.

The tunnel rises and falls, twists and turns. I stumble and trip too many times to count, my feet unsteady, my head throbbing from the rockslide. The mine feels like an endless maze we'll never escape, so I gasp when I turn a corner and I can make out grey, rocky outlines.

Rusty turns off the torch and we hurry towards the light. I keep one hand on the wall to steady myself.

"*The way out*," says Freddie proudly, confirming it's not my imagination.

To someone who's seen very little for what feels like hours on end, the daylight is as good as a rainbow. And it means we've still got time to stop the Cinderman.

The only thing preventing me from sprinting ahead are the sounds echoing down the tunnel from outside. The ashy wind is screaming, the ghosts *ooo*-ing and the ghombies growling. What is going on out there?

We all creep to the opening and stare out at the strangest game of tag I've ever seen; ghosts versus ghombies. The ghombies are mindlessly chasing after the ghosts, who have stolen all their digging equipment. Whatever was left of the buildings and sheds surrounding the mine is no more. The ghombies are picking up any missile they can, including bricks and bits of wood. They are pulling pieces of twisted metal out of the ground and hurling them at the ghosts, to absolutely no effect. Everything thrown just passes straight through the phantom bodies like stones through mist.

"*We sometimes have ghosts coming in here just to scare us,*" says Ivy. "*Like that Banshee. We hide from her. But I've never seen anything like this. It's like a penny dreadful come to life.*"

I can see the ghost girl better now in what's left of the daylight. She has long dark hair with matted ends and wears a torn grey dress. She reminds me of someone, but my brain can't make the connection. I'm preoccupied by the fact that I've got to go out there.

"They're all too busy with each other to worry about us," says Rusty, scanning the wasteland before pointing towards a tree stump. "We should make for that."

It's not too far away – about the same length as Dexter's garden.

"As long as we can make it without being seen," I say. "I'd really rather not get into a wrestling match with Banshee over the heart."

"*I'm afraid our part is done,*" says Freddie.

"*We can't leave this mine,*" adds Ivy. "*But you're going to stop him, aren't you? You won't let him hurt anyone else?*"

"I won't let him hurt anyone else." My voice trembles, but I mean every word.

"Thank you for helping us," says Rusty.

"*Ivy Hyde at your service,*" says the ghost girl, giving a little bow.

"*Freddie Blake,*" says the ghost boy. "*Pleased to have made your acquaintance.*"

"*Now's your chance,*" says Ivy.

She's right. I don't think the ghosts are doing it on purpose, but the battle seems to be moving away from the exit.

Rusty and I whisper hurried thank yous before sneaking onto the battle ground. We try to stay small and inconspicuous, Phrank scuttling alongside us, his feathers ballooning outwards like an upturned umbrella. I shove him under one arm before he's carried away by the wind, but we don't stop running until we reach the tree stump.

The sky is dark grey, a glimmer of pale, watery sunlight just visible on the horizon.

We still have time to reach the graveyard with the heart, but not much.

All around us are ghombies with torn and tatty clothes and ghosts with drawn faces and fuzzy outlines. Ash billows up from the ground, distorting everything. The landmarks I passed on the way here – from an old apple tree to tumbledown huts – have been ripped from the ground and for a moment I don't know which way to go.

Then I spot it – the great grey skeleton of Greyscar House.

"If we can make it there, we can find the route back to town and the graveyard," I shout to Rusty.

"What are we waiting for?"

We grit our teeth and run towards it, keeping low to the ground. I clutch Phrank for his sake and for mine. The warmth radiating from him is as comforting as a hot-water bottle.

By the time we reach Greyscar House, our lungs are heaving and we're spluttering in the ashy wind like goldfish out of water. We should keep moving – it's only a matter of time before we're spotted – but we need to catch our breath.

I put Phrank down and Rusty motions for us to creep around the side of the house. The timbers groan in the gale like a starving animal. My heartbeat quickens, but it's not because of the house. Something far more frightening is happening on the horizon. The sun is setting in the west, but directly opposite, to the east, I think I can see the moon rising.

We move away from the house in the dell and climb a rise to get a better view. It's not the usual vivid orange of a harvest moon, as the colour is dulled by the ash in the air, but it is climbing higher in the sky, signalling night's arrival and the beginning of the Cinderman's reign.

"We're going to have to run again," I say. "Are you ready?"

Rusty wipes his clammy-looking forehead with the back of his hand.

"I was born ready."

We take off down the drive, Phrank flapping alongside us. Thank goodness it slopes downhill towards the town because I don't think my legs could take much more punishment.

Rusty is channelling his inner Battle Beast again, going on

about harnessing "Arkiop courage" and "Varg stealth modes" – the only difference is that this time I join in.

When we finally sprint through the gates and onto Coal Road, I feel like we might actually have a chance. The graveyard is only a five-minute walk from here.

A roar splits the air, and the ground begins to shake.

I instantly feel less hopeful.

Unfortunately, the roar is just the start. Behind me, a town load of ghombies has just reached the top of the hill. I think I spot Miss Chen flanked by one of her Creep It Real tour groups. And behind them... I choke back a cry.

Silhouetted by sunset on one side and moonrise on the other is the Cinderman, all gnashing teeth and sharp claws set into a churning tornado of a body. He's sucking all the ash towards him, growing and swelling his hideous new form into something the size of Greyscar House.

"Now that's scarier than the Miasmic Swarm Lord," says Rusty, with a gulp.

I don't know what the Miasmic Swarm Lord is, but my stomach heaves and I throw up grey, ashy chunks onto the cinder-covered ground.

"*Ada,*" the heart murmurs fearfully.

It's right to be scared. I calculate we've got about ten seconds before we're toast.

23

Running has never hurt so much. Every part of my body is mad at me; my sides are burning, legs aching, throat drier than a box of crackers. I'm pretty sure Rusty and Phrank are feeling just as bad, but no one stops because, against all the odds, we've made it out of the mine with the heart. If we can just hold on a little longer, Little Hope Graveyard and Ada's grave are within reach.

Phrank is beside me, neck stretched out, wings wide, using every ounce of his strength to keep up even though pheasants aren't long-distance fliers. As we reach the metal entrance arch to the graveyard, he summons the strength to release a warning squawk.

There are two ghombies weaving between the gravestones towards us. One is wearing a tatty grey suit, the other an ash-stained flowery shirt.

We skid to a halt.

It's Mum and Dad. The white-eyed, teeth-bared, growling-like-a-rabid-dog versions.

At every stage the ghombies have been horrible, but this is something else. They sound hungry, like actual flesh-eating-type-zombies. The Cinderman has obviously dialled them up to level ten.

"Look, Mum, I'm wearing the boiler suit you bought me!" It's the first thing that comes into my head. I desperately want to make her happy, so she doesn't hurt me, but it doesn't seem to be working.

Mum hisses in reply and Dad fixes us with a white-eyed stare.

"Don't think Mum's keen to talk fashion right now, Indigo," says Rusty, stepping backwards.

"We need to separate them," I say.

"Divide and conquer! Great idea," says Rusty, with mock cheerfulness. "Let's Rock, Paper, Scissors it. Winner picks which parent they want to fight off!"

"I think they've already chosen..."

Mum is edging towards Rusty; Dad towards me. He's drooling saliva. If he decides to attack, I have nothing, not even a tissue, to fight him off with. And I really, really don't want to fight him. Somewhere, deep inside his horrible ghombie exterior, is the real Dad, the grumpy one who loves us and struggles to run the family business without Grandpa. I have to find a way to get through to him.

I take a deep breath. "I was reading one of the coffin brochures earlier – fascinating, by the way. I'm thinking of taking some classes..."

Is it me, or did Dad's eyes just give a flicker of recognition?

"...It looks like there are going to be coffin crafting workshops at the next Undertakers' Trade Show. I know I'm a bit young, but I was thinking..."

There's a hint of a smile on Dad's lips.

"...I was thinking you and I could sign up together. You know, spend some quality father–daughter time..."

He blinks. It's working. I'm getting through to him. And then he leaps for me. Unfortunately for him, I'm ready. I twist away and give him a good shove. His legs get tangled in the long, ashy grass and he lands with a yelp against a gravestone.

"This must be the worst family reunion in the history of family reunions!" yells Rusty. He's taken his long coat off and he's waving it around like a matador at a bullfight, only instead of dodging a charging bull, he's dodging a charging Mum.

"*Ada*," whispers the heart.

An iron determination settles in my chest.

My family drive me bananas, but the last thing I want is to lose them for ever. Look what happened to the Cinderman without his!

This is the fight of my life and I'm ready for it. There's no way Dad, Mum, or a whole ghombie army is stopping me from getting to Ada's grave.

Dad gets up from the ground, rolling his boiled-egg eyes and baring his teeth. He lunges at me again and I dart to the side, but he's quick and grabs one of the straps of my rucksack, yanking it so hard that I fall backwards.

I hit the ground with a thud, even though it's covered in ash, jarring my back and hitting every bruise I got in the mines. Before I can recover, Dad grabs my legs and starts dragging me back towards Greyscar House.

"Get off!" I yell, kicking out. Not that it does anything. He's got a firm grip. He doesn't even look back at me.

"Don't panic," shouts Rusty. "I've got this."

Suddenly, Mum appears with Rusty's coat somehow tied over her head. She crashes into Dad at full speed.

"Sorry!" Rusty yells as they both go flying.

As soon as Dad drops my legs, I'm on my feet. Arms pumping, heart hammering, I sprint through the graveyard. I can hear Mum and Dad snarling and growling like zoo escapees, but I can also hear Rusty. When I look back, he's yelling Battle Beast war cries from behind a gravestone and throwing ash balls at them. It hurts to leave him, but I tell myself he'll manage and force myself to go on.

I run deeper into the graveyard, tearing moss, ivy and grass from the headstones, desperately looking for Ada's name or the patch of honeysuckle. Some of the gravestones have collapsed, others are so wind blasted the names have been worn away. Even among the names I can read – Millicent Arbuckle, Pablo Grimes, Monty Freemangle – I can't find her.

Dexter and Sadie dash behind some yew trees, distracting me as I leap over the crypt sinkhole. Big mistake. A hand shoots out and fastens around my foot. I cry out as I crash to the ground. Miss Chen has somehow got ahead of me and fallen in here. She's standing on the shoulders of other ghombies, who are all wearing *Creep It Real* T-shirts. Her gold jewellery is jangling and her red nails glistening. She's using my leg as a rope, but instead of pulling her out, I'm being pulled down. It's like being stuck in quicksand – the more I fight, the further I seem to sink. My legs are now fully in the hole and her hands are nearly round my waist. One more yank and I'm done for.

With a squawk, Phrank lands on her head, pulling at one of her big gold hoop earrings. She tries to slap him away, but it makes the tower of ghombies below her wobble and she loses her grip on me. Phrank takes flight and the next thing I hear is a crash as the tower fully collapses and the ghombies hit the floor. My arms feel as weak as spaghetti as I heave my legs out of the sinkhole.

Phrank squawks at me to get a move on and so, even though my body is quivering and my breath coming in desperate gulps, I stumble on. I'm the one with the Cinderman's heart. I'm the only one who can stop this.

The roar of the Cinderman's ash fills my ears and I hear the screams of hundreds of ghosts as they urge me on. I must find Ada's grave before it's too late...

The silence is sudden and complete, like a switch has been flicked and the world has been paused. Gone are the growls of the ghombies, the howls of the ghosts and the cry of the wind. Even the ash has stopped falling; it hangs in the air as though suspended by invisible strings.

My mouth drops open. What's happened? Everyone and everything are frozen in time, except for the unholy trinity that is me and Rusty and the Cinderman.

Rusty runs to my side and together as Spooksmiths, we turn to face the enemy.

He's transformed from raging monster to man, the ash wrapping around him to form a three-piece suit, frock coat and top hat. He's six feet tall now instead of sixty and looks every inch the distinguished Victorian gentleman, with a cravat and neatly trimmed beard and moustache – all except for his eyes, which are dark, swirling craters of hell.

I can't speak. The only things moving are my thundering heart and the hairs on the back of my neck.

The ghosts are silent sentinels.

The ghombies frozen in time.

Mum and Dad are gurning; Miss Chen is reaching for Phrank, who is mid-flap; Sadie and Dexter are about to vault a tomb.

I could pick out at least fifty other people I know, including Ms Vago, Mr Cane and Mrs Maudlin. All these everyday faces aimed at me and Rusty, twisted with hatred and still as statues.

The Cinderman points to the east where the moon is rising.

"*Your time is up,*" his dry, ash-choked voice gloats.

A sinking feeling fills my stomach as I take it in. It's sunset. We've lost.

"*Ada,*" whispers the heart.

Beneath the stench of smoke and ash, the faint smell of honeysuckle drifts across the graveyard.

There's a flash of white.

Rusty grabs my hand as a ghostly girl with blond hair appears. She's standing beside the cliff-top grave I sat against only yesterday. It's Ada. Her blue eyes lock on to my brown eyes. There's an acknowledgement in them, a sense that she's ready to play her part. I finally feel like the tide might be about to turn in our favour and that awful tightness in my chest loosens.

The Cinderman is oblivious to the ghost of his sister, too focused on his own triumph.

He's smiling like it's all over, his ashy face rippling like a cluster of spiders.

"Are you going to let him win?" whispers Rusty.

"Over my dead body," I say.

Rusty grins, and before the Cinderman can react, I let go of Rusty's hand and race for the ghost girl beneath the rising moon. The Cinderman roars as he realizes what is happening. But nothing can stop me now. I pull back my arm and throw the heart to Ada.

24

For a moment, nothing happens. Bitter-tasting panic rises from my stomach and into my throat in a giant wave. Maybe I've got it all wrong. Maybe the ghost girl isn't Ada. Maybe uniting the heart with the Cinderman's sister wasn't the right thing to do...

And then, just as the heart begins its descent towards the ground, her hand shoots out and claims it.

Ada looks like an angel, all billowing white robes looped and twisted with honeysuckle – except for the beating red heart cradled in her hands.

The Cinderman's ashy face flickers and then freezes. It's as though he can't quite compute what is happening, like losing was never an option.

What is clear is that my part in this is over. All I can do now is hope that finding Ada has been enough.

So nervous I hardly dare to breathe, I join Rusty behind a broken gravestone to watch.

Ada walks towards her brother and the scent of honeysuckle fills the air. She extends a transparent hand, holding his heart out towards him. It's pumping in and out, as though her touch has brought it back to life.

"*Get away from me!*" he hisses. It's not clear whether he's talking about her, or the heart, or both.

He pulls his frock coat around him as though it will ward them off, but his coat looks less substantial than before, the edges fraying, buttons sagging. His heart, coupled with the appearance of his sister, is literally wearing his defences away.

"*I am not leaving without you, brother.*" Her voice is soft and willowy, but insistent, like a wind blowing through water reeds.

The Cinderman shakes his head.

"*I will never go with you.*" The words sound a struggle, like his throat is collapsing along with his suit, his shoes, his hair. Tendrils of smoke are streaming off him, as though his ashy clothes and his ashy skin are on fire.

"*You do not have a choice, Colton. You should not be here. Come with me.*"

Previously, speaking the Cinderman's name gave him

strength, but now the opposite seems to be happening and his shoulders sag.

"*This town is mine,*" he hisses, but his words are hollow threats.

Even from where I'm crouching behind the gravestone, it's obvious his hold on the town is faltering. The orange glow of the harvest moon is breaking through and the ashy haze surrounding Greyscar is clearing. The ghosts and the ghombies are unfrozen, and yet they don't rejoin the fight. They are as transfixed by the Cinderman and his sister as I am.

"*Let me help you,*" Ada pleads, extending her hand again.

"*No.*" His face twists in agony, as though it's taking every ounce of his strength to remain an ash monster without a heart.

Ada takes another step closer to her brother.

"*This town and these people are not yours for the taking. They never were and they never will be.*"

The Cinderman towers over her and yet she takes another step. Ada's ghost doesn't look much older than me, barely a teenager, but she doesn't flinch and she doesn't falter. Never taking her eyes from her brother, she twists away from him and then propels her fist forwards, punching her heart-holding hand deep into his chest.

The Cinderman staggers backwards.

"*What have you done?*" he wails.

Ada doesn't answer. She doesn't need to. When she pulls back her hand, she is no longer holding the heart. Instead, it's sitting in the grey, ashy cavity she made with her fist, glowing blood-red and alive.

The Cinderman reaches for his chest, but it's too late. Fragments of ash erupt from the hole, swarming out and away from the heart like angry bees from a wasp-invaded hive. It's as if all the badness is pouring out of him.

Ash is flying all around her, but Ada stands her ground.

"*I am here for you, Brother.*"

The Cinderman releases an ear-piercing wail. It's a heart-breaking sound, like an abandoned fox cub. His human form distorts, his clothes and limbs juddering apart as though his own heart is destroying him from the inside.

"*I feel everything! Make it stop!*"

"*It will be over soon,*" says Ada. "*What you are feeling is your conscience returning. To make amends, you must endure.*"

Ada takes the Cinderman's hand.

It crumbles to dust at her touch.

"*I am sorry.*" He exhales and what remains of his grey, ashy body and his blood-red heart explodes like a firework into the twilit sky.

The Cinderman's power over them gone, all the ghombies fall to the floor like dominoes. Rusty rushes over to check on Mum and Dad, but I stay staring at Ada because I don't quite believe it.

"Is it really over?" I ask, hands trembling.

"*It is over,*" she says.

"He won't come back?" I ask.

"*My brother will not trouble you again. All the anger and rage that fuelled him has gone. Feeling the emotions locked away in his heart has transformed him and enabled him to move on. I will meet him on the other side.*"

The stress and worry of the last few days peel away, and I clutch the side of a headstone, light-headed with relief.

"Will everyone be okay?" Rusty calls over from where he's sitting holding Mum's hand.

"*The townsfolk are asleep. When I leave, they will wake and remember nothing.*"

"Thank you," I stutter. "Thank you for helping us."

"*Thank you for helping me save what was left of my brother. My father twisted Colton into his likeness, made him hungry for only money and power. But we were close, once...*" She looks over at Rusty.

My brother is making sure Mum and Dad are comfortable, wiping the ash out of their faces and checking their pulses.

As far as brothers go, I guess he's not a bad one.

The wind gusts off the sea, fresh and salty, and Ada's ghost dissolves into it along with the rest of the ash.

There's just the ghostly army still standing. I come out from behind the gravestone.

Banshee, the terrifying screaming ghost of countless legends, is staring down at me as though she wants to ask me something. Finally, my brain makes the connection. The long dark hair and fierce stance give it away.

"You want to ask me if I met your daughter in the mine?"

Banshee nods her head once.

I smile. "Ivy Hyde is there. She helped me."

"*I have spent so long looking for her...and she appears for you?*" Banshee's hair spreads out to surround her pale face like a furious cobra flaring its hood.

I jump back, immediately seeing why Ivy might have been scared and hidden from Banshee. Her whole vibe doesn't exactly say warm and loving mother.

"You might look a bit different from how she remembers you when you were alive," I say carefully. "Do you think you could, you know, maybe not wail? The kids in the mine hide because they're frightened of you."

"*Frightened?*" says Banshee, like she doesn't understand the word.

Chuckles cackles and takes hold of Banshee's hand. *"She's asking you to be less screamy-scary."*

"You could maybe soften your look a little," adds Tanvir.

"Brushing your hair and changing that hideous dress would be a start," says Bernard, bluntly.

I roll my eyes. Typical Bernard.

All the other ghosts are now joining in with make-over suggestions and Banshee's looking more and more furious. I'm just thinking of a way to smooth things over, when I notice Banshee is still, shoulders relaxed, hair no longer standing out around her.

"How's this?" she asks.

Her dress isn't exactly clean, and her hair could still do with a brush, but she's different. Gone are the angry lines on her face and the haunted, desperate look in her eyes. She looks hopeful.

"Perfect," I say.

"Do you think Ivy will accept me now?"

"I do."

"Then I must go to her," says Banshee.

There's a gust of wind and she disappears and then one by one all the other ghosts disappear too. It's as sudden as blowing out a lit candle. One minute they're there, the next they're gone.

I'm guessing they've gone to help her find Ivy. That's going to be some reunion and I wish I could be there, but I've got my own family to worry about.

"Mum and Dad are waking up!" shouts Rusty.

I run over to the mossy grave they're lying on, pausing to move Phrank, who is perching on Dexter's head.

"Well done, bird," I say, ruffling his feathers.

I swear he gives a proud little purr.

There's nothing I can do for Dexter (now I've removed Phrank) other than wait. I have to trust in Ada that they, and all the other inhabitants of Greyscar, are going to be fine. Confused and with a few unexplained bruises, but fine.

I settle down beside Rusty and Mum and Dad. Before, all I wanted was to get away from them. Now all I want is to keep them close.

Dad's eyes open first, and he reaches for Mum's hand.

"I feel like I've forgotten something," says Dad. "Did I remember to take the bins out?"

The old Dad is well and truly back.

I grin and turn to Rusty. "We did it."

"It feels good to be a Spooksmith," announces Rusty. "But saving a whole town is exhausting!"

I smile and lean back against a tomb, bone-tired but elated.

The bats are returning to the belfry and there's a flash of orange as a fox flits out from behind the yew hedge. It clocks all the people waking up in the abandoned graveyard and scarpers. But I wouldn't run even if every part of my body wasn't aching. I'm exactly where I want to be. I'm with my family.

Grandpa was right, it's never too late to turn things around.

25

Five days later and Rusty is still the only person, besides me, who remembers anything about the Cinderman's ashy takeover.

There are loads of wild theories flying around as to how everyone ended up in the graveyard on that cold September evening. A few of my favourites are mass hypnosis, food poisoning and alien abduction, but there are a million more whacky theories in between.

Although, so far, no one has mentioned an urn of escaped ashes.

It's Saturday night and Rusty and I are sitting in the kitchen eating pizza, while Mum and Dad celebrate their anniversary at some fancy new Italian restaurant. The two of them haven't been out in ages. The old Dad would never take time off work and Mum wouldn't have trusted me and Rusty not to fight to the death. This is progress.

"You know Dad caught me talking to Mr Albatross's coffin," I admit.

Rusty snorts and puts down his slice of pizza.

"What did he say?"

"Mr Albatross said to remind his wife to water the petunias. Dad said if I'm interested in the 'other side', I should speak to the Rev." I sigh. "Still no word from Grandpa though."

I push the pizza away and pat my stomach. I should feel full. Things are good, if a little spooky with the whole being-able-to-commune-with-the-dead thing. It's just, I have a Grandpa-shaped hole in my life again.

"I hoped he'd be here when we got home," says Rusty.

"The Cinderman forced Grandpa outside when he took control of him," I say. "But he was a Category One ghost. He couldn't go outside."

There's an uncomfortable silence. Neither of us want to admit that Grandpa might be gone for ever.

"I miss him," I say.

"Me too," says Rusty.

I stare down at the half-eaten pizza. Rusty and I always eat the middles and leave the crusts. Unlike Dad, Grandpa never told us off for it. He said crusts were the best bit and would polish them off with a creamy garlic dip. It made his breath dead stinky, but I wouldn't complain about it now.

There's a faint buzzing sound and the lights flicker. My eyes meet Rusty's across the table.

"Did you see that?" My heart is racing.

"Uh-huh," he says with a grin.

They flicker again: on-off, on-off, on-off. Sometimes it's just a quick flash of light and other times they stay on for longer. I frown. It's almost like...

"Morse code!" says Rusty before I can.

Of course, it is! We both spent a summer learning it with Grandpa. All fired up, I jump up and grab a pen and paper.

"Dot-dot is I," I scribble. "Dash-dash is M."

"I again," says Rusty. "And two Ss."

The lights flash another six times and I keep writing. Then they stop.

I look down at the page and gulp.

"'I miss you too'," I read, my voice shaking with emotion.

"It's Grandpa! He's here!" says Rusty, spinning around.

But when I turn to look, the room behind me is empty.

"Where is he?" says Rusty.

The lights carry on flashing, and I count the dots and dashes, frantically scribbling down the letters. And then they stop again.

"What did he say?" says Rusty.

"'This is goodbye'," I read, a lump forming in my throat.

"No!" shouts Rusty. "No way! We've just found you again, Grandpa!"

The lights continue to flash, but I throw the pen down. I don't want to hear this. But Grandpa's taught me too well and even without writing it down I can work it out. And so can Rusty.

"He's saying 'pick up the pen'," says Rusty.

With a trembling hand I pick it up again and start to write, even though the page is wet with tears.

"'Top drawer of desk'," reads Rusty, over my shoulder.

We run to the funeral parlour and pull out the top drawer. Taped underneath is a set of numbers and instructions.

"'Second from the top, six along. One from the base. Seventh, fourth row. Ninth from the top'," reads Rusty. "Seventh, fourth row? It doesn't make any sense. It's gibberish."

But I know exactly what it is.

"It's the pattern to open the bookcase," I say. If he's giving us this, it really is goodbye, and I choke back a sob as the flashes continue.

Rusty grabs a pen from the desk and takes down the message. "'You have each other'," translates Rusty, his voice wobbling. "'I love you'."

We wait for more flashes. When they don't come, my loud, ugly sobs do. I can't hold them back and neither can Rusty. It feels good to let the loss out – "cathartic" is the word Mum uses in her counselling sessions. I even hold hands with Rusty. Briefly. When my chest stops heaving and the tears begin to slow, I wipe my eyes and I stand up.

"Are you okay?" I ask.

"Yeah," says Rusty, rubbing his nose on his sleeve. "I will be. Maybe we'll get to see him again one day."

"Maybe," I say.

It's a fact that ghosts exist, but the rest of the afterlife is a mystery. I'm happy to leave it that way. For now.

After lots of tears and serious amounts of ice cream to tackle our sore throats from crying, we're back in the crypt. We decided to tighten all the urn lids. There's no way another ashy megalomaniac is escaping with me and Rusty on duty.

"Everything looks secure," he says.

He flashes his torch along row upon row of metal urns, the contents muttering back at him as the light hits them.

I'm glad Rusty is here with me. Being a lone Spooksmith must be scary and isolating.

"Why does our family have these powers?" I muse. "Why us?"

"Because we can handle it," he says with a grin. "It might also have something to do with me being awesome enough to be the North East's Junior Battle Beast Champion."

I groan. He hasn't stopped going on about it. We all went along to support Rusty at the tournament yesterday evening. The Oldcastle conference centre was filled to bursting with kids watching other kids defeat armies of plastic models with a roll of the dice. Throwing a six is literally life or death. It was more fun than it sounds, not that I'd go so far as to admit that to my brother.

"Jai is so jealous I'm the Master Beaster," he says, pointing to the title on his prize T-shirt.

As if anyone could miss it. The words are written in red and dripping with blood. Beneath them, a gold monster that looks like a minotaur crossed with a T-rex battles a part-lion, part-snake-headed creature.

As he checks the urns at the far end of the bench, I turn my attention to the wall with the strange symbol: the circle containing a triangle with the letters V.S., M.I. and L.W. at each point.

"I don't buy that there isn't more to our powers and that someone, somewhere doesn't know more about it," I say.

"You know what Grandpa said: no one wrote anything down."

"Apart from this symbol," I say. "What do you think it means?"

There's a chirrup from the top of the stairs. It's Phrank, warning us that Mum and Dad are close to home.

My investigations into our Spooksmith powers are going to have to wait, but I'm determined to get answers.

We just have time to secure the bookcase behind us and run back into the kitchen, when Mum and Dad walk in.

"Did you have a nice time?" I say, trying to pose casually against the kitchen counter. If it's possible, Rusty is looking even more awkward than I am – he's standing ruler-straight beside the fridge.

"Lovely," says Mum, pulling off her coat.

Dad leans over and gives Mum a kiss on the cheek. It's a bit yucky, but it is nice to see them getting on well.

"What about you two?" Mum asks.

"What about us?" says Rusty. He looks decidedly shifty.

I mouth the word "Relax".

"Out with it," says Mum. "You're both behaving oddly."

"Did you two get in another fight?" asks Dad, his face tensing.

Rusty shakes his head.

"We were just talking about how much we miss Grandpa," I say.

Mum's face softens and Dad opens his arms. We both run into them like we used to with Grandpa, and Dad wraps his arms around us.

"I miss him too," Dad whispers into our hair.

"I'm not being left out of this," says Mum. "Let me in."

Dad lifts an elbow and Mum squeezes in. One big happy family. Until Phrank ruins it with a squawk.

"Phrank's not in the house again, is he?" asks Mum.

"You did say he could come in when it got cold…" I wriggle out of the hug. What Mum discovers next may mean I need to put a bit more distance between us.

"I said Phrank could come in the kitchen," says Mum, "but that squawk sounded like it came from the sitting room."

As if to prove her point, Phrank squawks again.

"He *is* in the sitting room!" says Mum.

"Indigo!" says Dad.

"What? It's not all my fault. Rusty was here too. He could have closed the door."

"You're blaming me for your pheasant?" says Rusty.

We're all arguing. Again. And I grin.

* * *

We're chasing Phrank around the sitting room – his key moves for avoiding capture are vigorous wing flapping and poo missiles – when the doorbell goes.

"I'll get it!" I dart back into the hallway and run through the funeral parlour to get the visitor door. It's strictly for customers, everyone else comes round the side. But Sadie doesn't know that.

Even though I suggested she come by so we could meet Dexter together, and so I could apologize properly for "Badgergate", it's still a shock to see her. The last time she was waiting for me she was a ghombie and things got dark pretty quickly.

"You're staring at my sneakers," she says, crossing her arms.

And I realize that yes, I am staring at her completely impractical white trainers.

"Sorry." I'm trying to be less judgemental and more easy-going, but old habits die hard. I take a deep breath and let it out. "You got the jumper bit right though. Forest green. Perfect camouflage."

There's a flicker of a smile on her lips.

"I'm really sorry I was so mean to you before," I continue. "I was worried you were trying to take Dexter away from me. I overreacted."

Sadie's mouth widens into a proper smile.

"I would never do that," she says. "I want to be friends with you both."

I blush, ashamed of how badly I've behaved. "Let me make it up to you."

There's a triumphant squawk from the sitting room followed by a lot of bad language.

"I've just got to help my family capture a pheasant first."

"I'll give you a hand," says Sadie.

Dexter's already at Little Hope Graveyard when Sadie and I arrive. He's set up a picnic rug and he's clutching a bat detector. He mouths "Shush" at us as we pick our way across the lumpy grass towards him. His bat detector gives off squeaks and clicks, although, of course, I can hear the bats without it.

One, two, three, four tiny creatures duck and dive over our heads.

Sadie looks nervously at them and pulls up her hood.

The old me might have sneered, but the new, improved version wouldn't dream of it. I'm a different person since the Cinderman and I realize what's important: family and friends. The new me is open to trying new things and isn't so quick to dismiss everything, however unlikely it may seem.

"You faced off against Phrank," I whisper. "A few little bats won't hurt you."

She nods and sits down on the rug, and I take a seat beside her. It's a clear night with the gentlest of sea breezes. When I next glance at her, she's taken down her hood and is staring upwards, spellbound by the bats' zigzagging flight. I'll make a proper animal lover of her yet.

We watch the bats until they finally fly off to new hunting grounds. Dexter switches on his torch and fills three tin mugs with hot chocolate from his Thermos flask.

"How about a quick ghost story before we go home?" says Sadie as Dexter hands the drinks round.

"I'll go first," I say.

He nearly drops his hot chocolate.

"You never tell ghost stories! You always pick them apart with scientific explanations and boring logic lectures."

I look towards the corner of the graveyard, at Ada's grave. The scent of honeysuckle has faded, the bloom gone from most of the flowers, but I know what happened here. I can hear the buzz of ghostly conversation echoing up from the crypt. Whether my friends believe me or not is up to them.

"Yeah, well ghost stories are usually a load of old rubbish," I say. "I've got a good one though."

"What's it called?" asks Sadie.

I grin.

"The Cinderman."

TOP SECRET

A Spooksmiths Guide

AKA what we've found
out so far...

SPOOKSMITH FACTS

- We're ghost-marked. It looks like a birthmark.

  Except it's not... The mark means that on our twelfth birthday we got an extra-special present: we could see and hear the dead. We're not Smiths any more. We're Spooksmiths.

- The good news: the mark protects us from evil ghosts.

- The bad news: the ghost mark skips generations and we don't know of any other families with it. We're on our own.

  Although we do have an animal sidekick...

  ghost prison

- There's a ~~trypt~~ underneath Serenity Funerals containing evil ghosts trapped in urns. Entry is through the bookcase. Code is: Second row from the top, six along. One from the base. Seventh, fourth row. Ninth from the top.

  Don't do an Indigo. DON'T DROP AN URN!

GHOST FACTS

- Ghosts stick around because of unfinished business.

- A ghost's real name has power.
  (the one they had when they were alive)

- The Cinderman had a physical tether to this world: his heart.
  Do all ghosts have a tether????

- Defeat an evil ghost by sunset.
  or wave bye-bye

- Stock up on salt, sage and lavender. They burn ghosts.
  I recommend Smell Fresh lavender air freshener for its excellent blasting capabilities.

- Ghostly powers are rated one to five:
  1. Category Ones like Grandpa are the most common ghosts, friendly but weak. They can't leave the place they died or touch things.

2. Category Twos like Chuckles, Tanvir and Ada can leave the place they died but there's a limit on distance. Can pick things up and cling to things but can't carry them around. Can't write or draw.

3. Category Threes like Bernard can do everything Category Twos can but travel further, carry stuff and write.

   If they're all like Bernard, then they're super grumpy.

4. Category Fours like Banshee are powerful and rare. Their powers include everything from the previous categories and more, like making the living hear their screams.

5. Category Fives like the Cinderman are all powerful. They can go anywhere, control the weather and zombify people.

   They are ultra strong, ultra rare and ultra angry.

Discover more Spooksmith facts in Indigo and Rusty's next spine-chilling adventure, as they travel on a railway for the dead and get lost in a ghostly mirror maze in a race to save their parents from a Victorian circus owner!

THE CIRCUS
OF SHADOWS

ACKNOWLEDGEMENTS

I'm grateful to so many people for getting me to this point. Dad, your blood-curdling bedtime stories were a highlight of my childhood and still haunt my dreams. Nick, thanks for hiding under the covers with me and the dogs. Mum, I'll always love you for keeping me in books with frequent trips to Thirsk library and for filling my life with an assortment of pets and four-legged companions.

To Lina Langlee, my amazing agent: without you none of this would have been possible. You are the best in the business. To my editor extraordinaire, Sarah Stewart, thank you for working wonders on my manuscript. You've made the whole process a joy. To everyone at Usborne, with special mention to Hannah Featherstone, Charlotte James, Gareth Collinson, Jacob Dow and Ayesha Mumal, thank you for getting on board with the Spooksmiths and getting it into the hands of readers. Kath Millichope, your designs are wonderful and Miriam Serafin, your beautiful cover art gives me goosebumps every time I look at it.

Big shout out to the WriteMentor team, especially Stuart White for setting up this glorious, accessible, and affordable writing community. Clare Harlow and Emily Randall Jones, I got so lucky the day you both chose to mentor me. Natalia Godsmark, Sarah Frend, Laura Collins, and Kristina Rahim thank you for being fabulous critique partners. Emma Read and Anna Britton for your guidance and editing services. Paula Wu Brooke thanks for helping me with Miss Chen and Jenny Chen Hazell thank you for lending your name. You did know I was doing that, right?

To Sara Grant, the SCBWI Undiscovered Voices team and their sponsor Working Partners, you gave this writer such a boost when I was on the verge of giving up. Also, my fellow UV 2022 finalists, Boot Campers 2024 and the #2024 debut group, thanks for the advice, laughs and support.

Peter and Jane, Catherine, Ben, Tom, Harry, Gay Blanchard, The Uni Girls, YLL, Puppy Chat and all my other lovely family and friends, thank you for still talking to me even when I cancel stuff because, "I'm writing".

Ellie and Edward, my brilliant children, who bicker just like Indigo and Rusty. Thank you for the inspiration, the cuddles and the belief that your mum could write a book. I love you both very much. Bill, thank you for all the rereads, notes, brainstorming, cups of tea and endless patience. I would be lost without you.

Finally, thank you reader for buying, or borrowing, this book and getting this far! I really hope we meet again.

ABOUT THE AUTHOR

Alex Atkinson loves scary books filled with oddball characters. She blames her idyllic North Yorkshire childhood spent playing murder-in-the-dark and listening to her dad's blood-curdling bedtime stories. After studying English and Politics at Newcastle University, she worked as a website content editor. She now lives in a village in Hertfordshire with her husband, kids and dogs, but dreams of abandoned buildings, ghosts and zombies.

SPOOKSMITHS INVESTIGATE: THE CINDERMAN is her debut novel.

WERE YOU SPOOKED BY

SPOOKSMiTHS INVESTIGATE

The CINDERMAN ?

LET US KNOW!

@usborne_books
@alexatkinsonstories
#TheCinderman